THE LIONS OF LOS ANGELES

A PARANORMAL SHAPESHIFTER ROMANCE

LILLY PINK

Get Yourself a FREE Bestselling Paranormal Romance Book!

Join the "**Simply Shifters**" Mailing list today and gain access to an exclusive **FREE** classic Paranormal Shifter Romance book by one of our bestselling authors along with many others more to come. You will also be kept up to date on the best book deals in the future on the hottest new Paranormal Romances. We are the HOME of Paranormal Romance after all!

* Get FREE Shifter Romance Books For Your Kindle & Other Cool giveaways

* Discover Exclusive Deals & Discounts Before Anyone Else!

* Be The FIRST To Know about Hot New Releases From Your Favorite Authors

Click The Link Below To Access Get All This Now!

SimplyShifters.com

Already subscribed?
OK, *Turn The Page!*

About This Book

When WereLion Evan McKay caught the scent of aspiring actress Lily Jones he knew that there would be trouble ahead.

Evan found Lily's scent to be irresistible and he knew he had to stop at nothing in order to claim her as his.

However, Evan was not the only WereLion in Los Angeles. The city was full of hundreds of lions just like him. Lions that would do anything they could to get a piece of this fresh piece of human meat also....

This is a paranormal shifter romance packed with action and red hot scenes filled with WILD amounts of passion. Download now to start enjoying this fun read!

CHAPTER ONE
CHAPTER TWO
CHAPTER THREE
CHAPTER FOUR
CHAPTER FIVE
CHAPTER SIX
CHAPTER SEVEN
CHAPTER EIGHT
CHAPTER NINE
CHAPTER TEN
CHAPTER ELEVEN
CHAPTER TWELVE
CHAPTER THIRTEEN
CHAPTER FOURTEEN

CHAPTER ONE

Lily did not like the look of the men hanging around her apartment building, not one bit. It was too dark to see their faces and she silently prayed that they would pay her no mind as she passed. There were three of them, youngish but with that street-hardened look that was all too common around downtown LA. They didn't seem to have any real reason for being there, and that thought nagged at Lily as she passed them.

Lily was in sweatpants and an old t-shirt, her unwashed hair done up in a haphazard ponytail. She was on a late-night run to the pharmacy down the street, a gesture of kindness for a friend apparently experiencing the worst cramps of the century. Tessa, unable to even leave her bed, had pleaded with Lily to go get medicine. Lily was not expecting any male attention in her current state, but the looks of the men by her apartment building were almost feral.

"Hey," one of them called to her after she had already passed.

Lily kept her eyes trained forward and her feet on pace.

"I said, hey."

The man jogged up to join Lily as she walked. Lily couldn't help but glance in his direction. He did not look as threatening as Lily had first thought. He had a sharp jaw line, made no less striking by his light facial hair. His strong features and natural tan skin would have looked more at home on a movie screen than loitering outside a Koreatown apartment building.

"Where are you going?" he asked.

Lily bit her lip and kept silent. Despite his looks, he could still be dangerous.

"I'd at least like to know your name."

He was walking closer to Lily's side, his arm nearly bumping hers as they walked. She thought about crossing the street to lose him, but he was blocking her way, whether intentionally or not. Lily slowed her pace. The man continued walking for a bit then turned around. His eyes flashed.

"You can't run, if that's what you're thinking."

Lily backed up, but the other two men were behind her. They pushed her in the back as the first man closed in at the front. They were pushing her towards the alley and she had no other place to go. Her feet stumbled as she continued backing away from them, farther and farther into the darkness of the alley.

The man who had been talking to her caught her by the arm. "We're neighbors. We should get to know each other." He pushed her roughly against the side of one of the buildings.

Lily wanted to scream but she was frozen. Her vocal chords were paralyzed, and she could not even choke out a plea to her attackers. The man leaned in close and took a deep, drawn-out sniff up her neck. He smiled.

"You have no idea just how special you are," he said.

Lily struggled under his grip, frantic to get free. But his strength was many times hers and her effort was futile.

"It's okay," he whispered into her ear, "you're going to come to like this."

Anger and disgust raged in Lily's chest and burned out her fear. She shouted straight into his eardrum and pulled her knee up between his legs. He clapped one hand to his deafened ear and the other to his crotch, losing his grip on Lily. She kept shouting at the top of her lungs for help, backing farther into the alley while keeping her incapacitated attacker between herself and the other two. When she safely reached the main street on the other end, she turned and broke into a run, not stopping until she reached the pharmacy.

A thin, tired-looking man was stocking a shelf near the front. Lily went up to him, out of breath and with a stitch in her side. Her dark hair was flying in all directions and her t-shirt was hanging low over one shoulder.

"I need you to call the cops for me," she panted.

The man only looked blankly at her through his thick glasses.

"Now!" she shouted.

* * *

Her scent was the first thing Evan noticed about her, that unmistakably female perfume that could not be faked or bought in a department store. It was a natural part of her, a special mix determined by her genes that drew him in like a lion to red meat. His animal blood surged inside his veins as it had not for some time. The beast inside of Evan had awakened, and there was nothing that would stop it from catching its prey.

He wound his way through the freshly-built film set, past big black cameras poised on dollies ready for the day's filming. He checked his reflection while passing the makeup station and was glad to see his wavy brown hair holding its shape even after a morning of tough rehearsals.

The crisp white shirt and navy jacket that costume design had put him in fit his muscled physique perfectly. He had worked hard to get where he was, not only in the gym but with his acting as well. He had survived the mean streets of LA to make it to Hollywood, never faltering in his determination to make something of himself. And it looked like he had finally succeeded.

Evan turned the corner, dodging his PA and a couple of the set crew as he closed in on his prey. She was standing in the bright studio lights, mumbling to herself as she read off a script clutched in her hand. Her dark hair was gathered into a messy bun, the woman clearly not having been through hair and makeup yet. Even so, her flawless skin had a healthy tan to it that Evan knew would read well on screen.

Evan evaluated her. Small-town girl, early twenties. *Probably her first time in the city,* Evan thought. The new ones are always hard to work with. Every so often she would half-gesture while reading the script as if thinking through her actions as she said her lines. *Over-rehearsing,* Evan thought with distaste. She would need a firm, experienced hand if she wanted to turn this gig into a career.

"Hey," Evan said as he closed the gap between them. Her blue eyes met his and the edges of her lips curled up before she had a chance to fully hide the extent of her delight.

He held out his hand to shake. "Looks like we'll be seeing a lot of each other," he said with a charming grin. "I'm Evan."

"I know," the woman replied. "I mean, it's nice to meet you. I'm Lily Jones." She looked embarrassed.

Today they were set to film the first scene between their two characters, and the director had wanted to make their first meeting on screen as genuine as possible. He would be furious that Evan was now sabotaging that plan. But he needed to figure out what was drawing him to her so strongly. As he shook Lily's hand, he continued to evaluate her.

"First time in Los Angeles?" he asked.

"Yeah," Lily replied. "I moved here from Nevada as soon as I got the role. I'm still kind of in shock."

Evan chuckled. "Don't worry, it'll pass. Where are you living?"

Lily toyed with a lock of her hair, seemingly hesitant to reply. "Koreatown," she said. "But only because it's close to the studio."

"And rent is cheap," Evan added. Lily blushed. "Don't worry," Evan smiled. "Everyone has to start out somewhere. But if you're ever in need of a hot shower with decent water pressure, you can come by my place."

Lily laughed at the half-joke, as if scared to believe that it might be an honest invitation. As she laughed, Evan could not help noticing the low cut of her loose v-neck tee. Though clearly something she had thrown on with little thought this morning, it flattered her figure well and gave Evan just enough of a hint at what it hid beneath to drive him crazy.

Lily looked down at her script about to say something, but one of the PAs came running up telling her to get to hair and makeup.

"Guess I've got to let you go," Evan said as he watched the PA disappear back into the chaos of the set. He was already backing away from Lily, establishing the direction of the chase. The best hunters knew how to get the prey to come to them. If he always left her wanting more, she would come to him herself in no time.

"Oh, and don't tell the director we've met." He winked. "See you later."

As he turned away, her scent still lingered in his nostrils. Evan was a man, but with the blood of a lion, able to assume either form with equal ease. He was a shape shifter, in more common terms. And it was the animal side of him that knew instantly that Lily possessed the right genes to produce the strong, healthy offspring his pride needed. Of course, capturing her would take time. And he would have to do it before any of the other lions got a whiff of her.

* * *

The lights seemed off. Too bright maybe, or she just was not used to all this attention on her. Or maybe she was still shaken by the attack in the alley the other night. The flame-colored eyes of her attacker sent cold chills through her body every time she remembered them. Lily tried to push such thoughts out of her head and focus on the scene. She kept telling herself to pretend that she had never met Evan, though it seemed obvious that the director knew about their short conversation earlier that day.

Everything seemed to be falling apart. Except, of course, Evan who was doing his professional best to carry her through the scene. She hoped he knew that she was apologizing profusely in her mind.

"Cut!" the director yelled, making Lily jump. He leaped off his chair and made a beeline for Lily. She pressed her damp palms against her thighs, waiting for the worst. The short, clean-shaven man put an arm around Lily's shoulders and pulled her in close. "Sweetie, I'm so sorry I paired you up with this moron," he gestured toward Evan. "He keeps missing his marks and that's putting you off. Don't worry, it's entirely his fault. You're lovely."

The knot in Lily's chest dissolved at the director's kind words. She gave a small smile to Evan, but not one of apology. It seemed even experienced actors could make mistakes. She felt the color return to her cheeks.

"And you," the director said, releasing Lily and whacking Evan on the arm. "If I didn't know any better, I'd say you've caught the love bug. Maybe if you stopped ogling your costar, you'd be able to hit your marks."

Evan dismissed the director with a wave of his hand. "We're just meeting each other for the first time, right? So, it's only natural that things are a little awkward. You're the one that wanted authenticity."

"If you don't hit your marks, we won't be able to see your authenticity on screen."

"Adjust the cameras then."

"Don't tell me how to do my job."

Lily watched Evan as the two argued pointlessly. It seemed surreal that a man like him could be only feet away, a rising star who seemed to come out of nowhere but was now contending for the hearts of millions of female fans. Lily wondered if the same would happen to her, a girl from the desert of Nevada. But she could definitely see Evan's charm, whereas her own was still elusive to her.

Though pairing known actors with undiscovered gems was all the rage in Hollywood these days, Lily didn't feel like a gem. She felt like a lost girl who had accidentally wandered onto set. Here were people like magazine covers walking all around her and all she could do was stare. Why she had been picked for such a role was still beyond her imagination.

"Sorry about that," Evan said suddenly, bringing Lily out of her reverie. He had rolled up his shirt sleeves to his elbows, exposing his strong wrists and forearms. If they got this scene down, those arms would soon be around Lily in their very first onscreen kiss.
His light, almost golden eyes regarded her with kindness. "I won't miss my marks this time."

When they started shooting again, Lily felt like she floated through the scene, buoyant on the kind words of the director. Evan hit his marks, as promised, and the scene was wrapped earlier than expected. The triumph of finishing her first scene was only slightly overshadowed by Lily's realization that the day had already flashed by. Even with the quick turnaround, they were running behind schedule and there would be no time for the kiss today.

As she made her way to the cast and crew trailers parked outside the studio, Evan jogged up beside her. "Something on your mind?" he asked, playfully nudging her shoulder. He fell into step next to her, nodding at the staff as they passed.

Lily envied how comfortable he was on set, and how familiar he was with the staff and directors. Lily never knew if people were being genuinely friendly towards her or just being polite because she was the main female lead.

"It gets easier, right?"

"The job? Yeah. Or, at least you grow a thicker skin. The director seems to love you. And I sure don't mind sharing screen time with a woman as beautiful as you."

Those buttery words that Lily had heard often from the mouths of agents, directors, and those otherwise trying to get something out of her, fell flat against her ears. Show business was full of fake compliments and smiles. It was the only way to keep going in an industry run by connections rather than talent. She smiled but declined to respond.

"Hey," Evan said as they neared Lily's trailer. "We never got to that kiss."

She stopped. "Yeah, I guess not."

Evan stood close to her, his hand on her trailer door, pressing it closed. He leaned in and, cupping her cheek with his strong hand, touched his lips to hers. It was like fire inside of her, and though she wondered if this too was just an act, she kissed back with equal passion.

His hand moved from the door and slid up the outside of her shirt, though its heat could be felt through the thin fabric. His hand found the swell of her breast as his tongue entered her mouth. She was weak in his grip, ready to let him do anything to her. It was an almost hypnotic hold he had over her. She had never felt anything like it before.
But all too soon, the intense heat of Evan's lips left hers and she was left with only her heart thudding hard in her chest.

She didn't know what to say. Evan only looked at her expectantly.

"I'm sorry," she finally managed. "It's, um, been a long day."

Evan laughed. "Don't worry, I caught you off-guard. I just couldn't help myself."

Lily smiled shyly as she opened the door to the trailer, and Evan started towards his own trailer without further comment. Lily wondered what the kiss had been about. There was nothing stopping her from hooking up with her costar, but it just had not seemed like an appropriate time. After all, they had only just met.

As soon as the door closed, Lily collapsed against it. She stood leaning against it as the day's nerves washed out of her system. Suddenly, she was exhausted. Everything seemed like a dream, as cliché as that was. Lily knew that coming to Hollywood would be nothing like what she had imagined back home, but transitioning from skeleton crew indie movies to kissing movie stars in massive studio lots in less than a year was going to take a lot of adjustment. And that was only her work. She knew there was still a whole other world waiting for her at her apartment.

The traffic in LA alone was bad enough. She had thought living in Koreatown would be close enough to Hollywood to make her commutes a piece of cake. But what she hadn't accounted for was the real nightmare of LA traffic. Nor had she realized that not all parts of Koreatown were suitable for a single young woman to live in.

The apartment owner had apparently taken advantage of Lily's inexperience in LA and her desire for affordable rent, and had not informed her of just how dangerous her neighborhood was. *Maybe all big cities were this way*, Lily thought, and she would get used to it over time. But for now, she would have to stay on guard.

She unbuttoned the front of her blouse and shrugged it off her shoulders. She then went to the clothing rack and hung the blouse on an empty hanger, taking her v-neck from where she had hung it previously. The trailer was comfortably furnished with a sofa, TV, table, and a small refrigerator where Lily had already stashed her secret tube of chocolate chip cookie dough.

It would come in handy on long shooting days when Lily needed the energy and moral support. For now, all she wanted was a hot shower and a good night's rest.

After slipping out of her jeans and into some stretchy but form-fitting black pants, she left her trailer to head home. Most of the crew were still buzzing about, prepping for the next day's shooting and doing whatever it was that they did to help create movie magic. Evan was nowhere to be seen.

Down the block, Lily sat in her beat-up car trying to coax the engine to life. It coughed and hiccuped and went dead. She pounded on the wheel and cursed the hunk of metal, letting loose strands of her hair fall over her face and make her look like a wild woman. She took a deep breath and tried again. Finally, the engine sputtered to life and Lily jammed it into gear. Tires squealed as she pulled out onto the street.

Luckily, she had missed the worst of the traffic, and her drive home took less than an hour. She knew her roommate would be home already, her best friend Tessa who had been crazy enough to move with her to LA. Tessa worked in marketing and could take her work anywhere. She was also the type to keep no strings attached romantically.

Lily suspected that she had left Nevada to avoid impending commitment. While Lily also liked to keep things light, she always had it in the back of her mind that if she found the right man she would settle down. The problem was, there were no right men.

Because of the chronic lack of parking in her neighborhood, Lily was forced to park a few blocks away from her apartment. Though in the light of day this distance was not particularly inconvenient, it made a world of difference at night. Her neighborhood was full of bars, good food, and a particularly rowdy weekend crowd.

But the block of her apartment was shrouded in a special kind of darkness that the distant echoes of booming dance music and laughing voices couldn't penetrate. Like a scene straight out of a horror movie, the street light at the corner of the block was about ready to go out, its blinking light illuminating broken bottles and smashed cigarette butts on the street below in an erratic Morse code signaling danger.

As Lily passed a group of guys walking the other way on the sidewalk, only feet from her front doorstep, one of them turned his head to look at her. There was an intensity in his eyes that worried her, more than just a passing interest. When he started to follow her, she walked faster, not daring to look back to see if he was still behind her. She ducked into the entryway of her apartment building and let out a deep breath, hearing the door close soundly behind her. Only then did she turn around to make sure he hadn't followed her inside.

Maybe she was being paranoid, but it was better to be safe than sorry. The wail of police sirens was far from rare in her part of the city. To be fair, much the same could be said about any part of LA, except perhaps the ritzy multi-million dollar neighborhoods of Beverly Hills or any other place A-list celebrities liked to frequent. In any case, Lily did not expect to be out here too much longer.

As she waited for the elevator up, the front door opened with a rush of air. Lily jumped and her head snapped toward the open door, ready to make a run for the fire stairs in back. But the pleasant tinkle of laughter calmed her instantly.

"Jesus, that was quite the reaction. Too bad I didn't get it on camera." The blond woman walked towards Lily and hooked an arm around hers. "How was your first day?"

Lily let out a sigh as she rested her head against Tessa's shoulder. "I'm exhausted and I have no idea what I'm doing. But I kissed Evan McKay."

Tessa replied as she watched the light above the elevator make its slow descent to the first floor. "How many times did you have to re-shoot the scene? I know if it were me, I'd have screwed up on purpose."

"We didn't even get to that scene," Lily said with a small, self-satisfied smile. She couldn't wait for her friend's reaction. "He kissed me outside my trailer."

The elevator dinged and the doors slid open. Tessa stared at Lily incredulously as they entered the elevator together. "You kissed him, or he kissed you? It doesn't matter. You've got to hit that. I mean, I know he has a reputation but you can't pass up an opportunity like this."

Lily waited for Tessa to calm down before replying. "He kissed me. And I probably could have invited him into my trailer, but it was all so much for the first day. I didn't want to complicate things even more."

The elevator stopped on the fourth floor and the two women got out. Tessa fished through her oversized handbag as they walked down the hall, not realizing that Lily already had her apartment keys in her hand.

"Well, you can't—shit." There was a sound like paper ripping as Tessa searched more furiously for her keys. "I mean, you can't wait too long. Guys like that lose interest, you know? They're easily distracted by a pretty face."

Lily unlocked the door and Tessa abandoned her search with a sheepish smile. The apartment they shared was small, but surprisingly clean and cozy. The two of them had worked hard on the interior decoration, trying their best to disguise the less attractive features of their cheap apartment. Lace curtains hung over the windows looking out onto the street, and a luxurious shag rug covered the questionable carpeting of the living room space.

Vases of fake but convincing flowers added a little green to the room with minimal maintenance.

Lily put down her own reasonably-sized purse and coat on the sofa and went to the fridge. She took out ingredients for dinner, setting them on the counter as she talked.

"Even if he does get distracted, it's not like he's the only good-looking guy in all of LA," she said to Tessa, who had begun shucking off her clothes as soon as she had entered the apartment.

22

The woman was currently in her bra searching for a clean t-shirt. Tessa hated clothing in general, and was always happy to exchange her skinny jeans for a pair of boxer shorts and a loose t-shirt whenever she had the chance.

She probably would have walked around naked had Lily not put a firm stop to it. Lily loved her best friend, but she didn't want to think about her friend's bare bottom every time she sat down on the sofa. It was an issue of sanitation.

"That reminds me. We should go out this weekend. We haven't had a chance to celebrate coming here yet," Tessa said as Lily put a pot on the stove to boil pasta.

"What are you thinking? A club?"

"When am I not thinking about clubs?" Tessa replied.

Lily laughed. "I want to go somewhere really nice. Like somewhere movie stars would go."

"Got it," Tessa replied. "I won't disappoint you."

CHAPTER TWO

Evan let out a wide yawn as he stretched out on his rooftop patio in the warm LA sunshine. If he were to be perfectly honest, he was renting the place entirely for its roof access. The apartment itself was quite small, but there were few greater joys in life than basking in the sun on a particularly lazy Saturday afternoon.

Below him, the city bustled under the summer rays, cars stretched out in lines trying to get to the 101, the north-south highway that ended in the traffic nightmare of downtown. Evan yawned again, sleepy from the heat on his golden fur.

Evan loved his lion form. It was the powerful, primal side of him that fueled his desires and drew women to him. Of course, he did not divulge his secret to any of his short-term flings, but nevertheless it was his animalistic nature that they picked up on and responded so eagerly. It was on this allure that he would have to rely to get Lily as his mate.

His phone rang atop the pile of clothes it was resting on. It was his father. He begrudgingly shifted back into his human form and pulled on his clothes. The phone continued to ring, as Evan knew it would, no matter how long he took to answer it.

"Hello?"

"Evan, you're not working today."

"No, Dad. It's the weekend."

"You didn't send the rent check."

"I did, three days ago. I even called your landlord to make sure he got it."

"No, I meant your brother's."

Evan sighed. "I didn't know I was paying my brother's rent. What happened to his construction job?"

"He got in another fight."

Evan's hand clenched into a fist. His older brother, Matt, could never seem to hold down a stable job. Matt had been rebellious in his youth, and in defying the authority of his father, fell in with a rival pride. Those lions were the ones that had gotten Matt into hard drugs and petty crimes. Matt spent most of his teenage years in and out of juvenile detention centers, and on more than one occasion, Evan had to come to his defense.
He still had the scars.

"Okay," Evan said to his father. "Send me the rent bill and I'll take care of it. But you know I can't keep doing this."

"It was your choice to carry the responsibility of the pride. You can't give it back. Just because you're a movie star now, it doesn't mean you can turn your back on us."

Whenever the pride needed something it was their alpha they looked to. Evan wished he had never chosen to challenge his father to become the dominant male of their pride. He should have waited until Matt cleaned up and took the responsibility for himself.

Evan replied, "I'm not turning my back. I'll pay Matt's rent as long as he needs. But tell him he'd better get a job soon or I'm telling his wife where his rent check's coming from."

At that, his father laughed. The sound took some of the tension off the call. "You're a good son," he said. "I'm glad you're the alpha."

Evan debated telling his father about Lily, but decided to wait until he saw the man in person. Instead, Evan said goodbye and hung up. It was too important to discuss over the phone.

Plus, there were other things to worry about now. If Evan did not cut back on his own spending, he would have to find another way to make some extra cash until his brother found a job. On the streets where he grew up, there were plenty of ways to make money, as his brother had found out at a young age, but returning to that life would be dangerous.

He would have to go back to the underside of LA, to the shadows that he had worked so hard to escape from. He hated the idea, but the pride as a whole was more important than his own selfish desires. He promised himself to stop spending so much money.

* * *

Lily's scare last week was all the more reason to go out tonight, at least according to Tessa. Lily herself was not so sure. Before going out, she had grabbed a gauzy black cardigan off a hanger in their shared closet and draped it over her shoulders. Her sleeveless blouse had been making her feel more exposed than she would have liked, at least for now. Inside the club, it would be no problem.

Tessa stood beside her in line, craning her neck around at all of the well-dressed people around them.

"I don't see anyone famous," Tessa pouted. "And this place looks like an old theater, but not in a good way."

Lily gave a cursory glance around. "I don't think anyone famous would be stuck waiting in line, and it *is* an old theater. There's a lot of history to this building."

"I don't care about history," Tessa replied.

"Just wait until we get inside. Besides, you're the one who chose this place."

They were standing outside the Avalon, a massive nightclub in Hollywood that catered to both the regular weekend party crowd and VIPs who had a guest list-only space upstairs. Lily hoped that one day she would be able to get on that list, but for now she was stuck waiting in line with her increasingly impatient best friend.

"Li—ly," Tessa nagged, pulling on Lily's arm, but Lily was too busy studying the intricate façade of the historical theater to pay her friend much mind. "Lily, isn't that the guy in your movie? What's his name, Evan McKay?"

Lily spun around and looked down the line of people, suddenly extremely nervous.

"No, over there."

Tessa was pointing away from the line, to a man walking up the sidewalk towards them. Even as he turned away to wave at someone he knew in line, Lily could tell it was Evan. He noticed her and jogged up.

"Hey, Lily. I didn't expect to see you here."

Evan's slicked-back hair and button down with its sleeves rolled up gave him a classic movie star look that Lily loved. He looked like he had just walked out of a film reel. Of course, he was still not quite famous enough to create an onrush of fans wherever he went, but Lily could still hear whispers from those around her as if they may have recognized his face.

She did her best to act calm. "This is my friend, Tessa," she said, gesturing to her friend who seemed to have lost all capacity for speech.

"Hi, Tessa," Evan smiled. He turned back to Lily. "How long have you two been waiting in line?"

"Not too long," Lily replied.

"Twenty minutes," Tessa corrected, apparently having found her voice again.

Evan laughed. "Why don't you guys come with me? There's a private space upstairs, Bardot, and I just happen to be on the list."

Lily hesitated to accept. "I'm not sure—"

Tessa interrupted. "It's kind of you to offer, but I came here to dance like crazy in a room full of sweaty people. I have a feeling that VIP lounge of yours is a bit too quiet for my tastes."

Evan laughed again. Lily marveled at his easy nature. With Tessa, it had none of the sharp, almost aggressive edge it had with her. With Tessa, he was just being nice. With Lily, it always seemed like he wanted something from her.

"Don't worry, I can get you in there, too. So, what do you say?"

Tessa nudged Lily's arm.

"Yeah, OK," Lily replied. It sure beat waiting outside and paying the cover charge. And she could not deny that the memory of his kiss was still fresh in her mind.

"Great," Evan said, and they left the line together, following him around the building to a separate entrance used only by those with reservations.

Evan gave his name to the man at the door and the three of them were let inside. The space was massive. Past the lobby and VIP booths, Lily could see the main dance floor. At the front was a raised DJ platform that shone strobes of light over the wild crowd. Bass boomed from the speaker stacks on stage as people pushed their way through the crowd to get to the bar.

Most people were dressed rather casually, apart from those lounging at the booths who had shelled out for bottle service. A man in a sharp suit came in from the entrance they had used and headed upstairs. Lily couldn't shake the feeling that she had seen him in a magazine somewhere.

Lily slipped off her cardigan and folded it over her arm.

"Not my scene. Let's go upstairs," Evan half-shouted into Lily's ear.

Lily relayed the message to Tessa, who had already started wandering towards the bar. Tessa took the opportunity to pull Lily aside.

"Private lounge, just the two of you. You know what this means, right?" Tessa's eyebrows raised expectantly.

Lily waved her away. "Stop it."

"Okay," Tessa said with disappointment, "but you're wasting your youth, you know."

Lily stuck her tongue out at Tessa and disappeared into the crowd. She rejoined Evan and they made their way upstairs.

Upstairs was an entirely different vibe. The Bardot lounge had an old-fashioned but glamorous feel, with intimate lighting from candles and chandeliers, and ornately carved doorways leading from the lounge and bar area to the small stage. Well-dressed people sat on the velvety dark sofas, over which reproductions of classical paintings hung.

They sipped drinks and chatted with one another, a few looking up and nodding at Evan as he entered. The soft croon of a female jazz singer trickled in from the stage in the adjoining room. Tonight seemed to be nothing special in particular, but Lily was in awe nonetheless. She ached to be one of these people who lived such beautiful lives, to belong in these surroundings instead of feeling like a trespasser. She wondered if Evan had always belonged, or if he too had come here first as an outsider.

He didn't give her long to ponder that thought. "Here, drink this."

Lily had not even realized Evan had left her side, but he was now holding two tall glasses of a pale, bubbling liquid. She accepted the glass and took a sip. It was like heaven.

"I probably can't afford this, you know," Lily said with a self-conscious smile.

Evan slipped his hand around her waist and led her to one of the velvet sofas. "Maybe not now, but soon."

They sat for a while drinking and chatting pleasantly, but soon enough their conversation faltered. Besides their shared work, there did not seem to be anything in common between them. Lily tried asking Evan about his life before acting, but the man was strangely evasive. Either he felt uncomfortable having grown up with a silver spoon in his mouth, or he was hiding something unpleasant.

Either way, Lily was struggling to connect. It was as if Evan had built a wall around himself, and every time she approached it, he pushed back hard. Just how many secrets was he hiding?

Evan stood up suddenly. "Let's go downstairs, just for a little while."

Lily set down her glass. "I thought it wasn't your scene."

"I'll make an exception just this once. For you."

Something about Evan's smile told Lily he was no stranger to the anonymous grinding of the dance floor, but she only smiled and followed him downstairs. She was more than glad to escape the awkwardness of their dead conversation.

After that, the night went by in a blur of dancing bodies and flashing lights. Evan stayed close to her, his body moving against hers in rhythm with the beat. Though the space was crowded and chaotic, she and Evan carved out their own intimate space, communicating through touch as their voices would not carry.

She caught his eye, smiled, then turned away again, intoxicated by the music and heat of growing attraction. His face lit up with the blues, greens, and reds of the spotlights coming down from the stage as they danced. Close to him, she could even smell his pleasant cologne over the dance floor haze of sweat. At every move, he was there, never wandering and never letting her get lost in the sea of random people.

Though other men tried to dance with her, it was always Evan that she found herself with, his movements matching hers in an almost instinctual way. It was as if their bodies were meant for each other, and they connected in a way they had not been able to through words.

When they finally made their way back upstairs, most of the crowd had thinned out. Lily sank down into a low booth. Evan sat down next to her.

"Have you ever seen the sunrise over the Hollywood hills?" Evan asked.

"No," Lily replied.

"Then, let's go. There's not much time until sunrise."

Evan took hold of her hand and Lily had no time to catch her breath. Lily followed him out of the lounge, still giddy from the night but feeling a new, fresh kind of exhilaration on top of it that had nothing to do with the alcohol she had consumed hours earlier.

Hand in hand, they wove past the slow, zombie-like stragglers left in the club as things died down. She felt as if they were the only two truly living. Outside on the street, the darkness was just starting to thin, only a hint of the approaching dawn visible to those looking for it.

Evan led her to his car and opened the passenger door for her. He gently helped guide her down onto the seat, his strong hand holding hers like a prince in a story book as she sunk down into the soft leather. The car was old, she could tell that much, but lovingly cared for. A classic. Something told her he had bought it cheap and fixed it up himself.

"You okay?" Evan asked as he slid into the driver's seat next to her.

"Yeah," Lily nodded. "Where are we going?"

Evan pulled out onto the empty street. "It's not well-known, but it's a little lookout point that's got a great view of the Hollywood hills. You won't be able to see the sign, because that's better at sunset."

Evan fell silent as he drove through the sleeping city. Lily watched out her window, pondering how different it all looked without the cars and people. *It was not so scary after all,* she thought. Just buildings and palm trees. They had the same in Nevada. Bit by bit, this town would become hers.

It would become just as familiar as the streets of the tiny neighborhood she grew up in, where she and Tessa would dress up and put on plays for their parents on those long summer days that were the start of Lily's dreams. Lily sighed and smiled dreamily out at the slowly approaching dawn. She dozed, but for how long she did not know.

The crunch of tires on gravel woke Lily and she sat up just in time to hear the engine cut and feel Evan's hand on her knee.

"We're here," he said.

Lily stretched and looked out at the view. They were on a small plateau that looked out over LA and past it, the mountains. Even in the darkness of pre-dawn, the view was breathtaking.

"How much time?" she asked.

"It's hard to tell. But it's already getting light."

She bit her lip. "I don't know what I'm supposed to do," she said.

"What do you mean?" Evan asked.

"Now, with you. You took me out here to watch the sunrise, but is that really it?"

Evan's hand shifted higher on Lily's leg.

Lily placed her hand over his. "I don't know what to do."

"You do what you want."

His words came out like a secret whisper from within Lily's own chest. It was clear Evan wanted her, but he wanted to tease her, too.

He was making her come to him, driving her crazy until she would surrender to her lust. She was too nervous to make the move herself.

Evan leaned over Lily and kissed her. It was just as electric as their first, but with more intention behind it. Their first had been an invitation, a taste, a tease. This one was more forceful. It was a command.

She pulled Evan closer, feeling his hand slide up past the hem of her skirt. The fabric rode up over her thighs as his hand moved further. He gave a gentle bite to her lower lip, just enough to show his dominance. His lips moved to her ear.

"You have no idea how crazy you make me."

Lily pushed him back into the driver's seat and straddled him, feeling the hot urge to take him inside of her. The close quarters of the car's front seat and the steering wheel against Lily's back were pushing their bodies against each other, encouraging the inevitable with a forceful hand. Lily tugged at Evan's shirt, and he let her peel it off him.

Evan then slipped Lily's shirt over her head and his hands unclasped her bra. Her bare flesh pushed against his, their shared heat raising steam that fogged the edges of the windows.

Growling with lust, Evan slid his hands up Lily's thighs and pushed aside her panties. Lily fumbled to unzip his jeans below her, her movements hurried and needy. As she struggled with the zipper, Ethan reached over her to the glove box. Lily rolled the condom down over his member slowly, letting him ache with anticipation.

He swore under his breath, barely able to restrain himself. Lily didn't know how long their fling would last, but she wanted it to be good while it did. She wanted him to remember her. After all, he wasn't just another one-night screw—he was her costar.

He pulled her down on top of him, letting his length fill her. They fell into a fast rhythm. Lily closed her eyes, focusing on the realness of his skin against hers and his heat inside of her. *This was really happening*, she told herself. This was not some Hollywood magic, some dream of film made on a movie set. Evan was real, and he was, for however short a time, completely hers. Lily could feel the warm rays of sunlight against her arched back. She opened her eyes to see the back of the car illuminated in golden light. The sunrise.

But she was far too distracted to appreciate it now. Evan gathered up Lily's hair in one hand and pulled it upwards, exposing her neck to his teeth. He bit to the brink of discomfort, then kissed the tender spot. Lily whimpered, her body tightening as waves of pleasure washed over her. Evan stiffened below her and let out a primal growl.

"I missed it, the sunrise," Lily said as she settled down into the passenger seat.

Evan, still breathing hard, wiped sweat from his brow. "Then I guess we'll just have to do it again sometime." He winked.

Lily gave him a look and got busy pulling her shirt back on. She gazed out the front windshield at the city already awash in the first rays of morning. She didn't want to go back to her apartment. She wanted to stay with Evan in this dream world he inhabited.

She imagined his home as a clean, spacious penthouse apartment with a wide balcony overlooking the city. More than anything, she wanted to go there and lie in the big, soft bed she imagined him owning, losing herself in the high-thread count sheets until the sun passed its noontime peak.

Evan planted a kiss on her cheek and put the car into gear. Gravel crackled under the tires as he pulled away from the overlook point, back towards the quickly heating city. Though only June, the summer was already starting to sizzle. Of course, nothing compared to the Nevada heat Lily was used to, but much of LA was paved with black asphalt that stored the sun's heat and made the city seem that much hotter.

Evan cracked the windows as he drove, letting in a breeze that ruffled Lily's hair. She leaned back and closed her eyes, sleepy and content, and perhaps starting to fall in love.

It was only when she got home that she realized she had left her sweater in Evan's car.

* * *

"I found her." Evan paced the peeling linoleum floor of his father's apartment with his arms folded across his chest. "The mate that this pride needs."

His father leaned against the kitchen counter with a beer bottle in his fist, his Dodgers jersey ballooning out over his gut. He had been tough, almost ruggedly handsome, in his early days but the long years had worn him down.

"You've been spending too much time around movie stars and models," the older man said in his gruff voice. "You don't know what you're talking about."

Evan stopped pacing. "If you met her, you would know. She's the one. And if the others haven't caught her scent yet, they soon will."

Evan's father scratched the stubble on his cheek. "You're going to get yourself into trouble, you know, chasing after women like gazelles on the safari. And when you finally stop thinking with that idiot in your pants and realize your mistake, it'll be too late. You'll have soiled the pride with a bunch of weakling cubs, and a mate you don't even care for."

Evan wished he could do something to convince his father, short of introducing him to Lily. He knew his instinct about her was right. If only his father could see it.

The older man continued. "When I met your mother, I knew she had the blood. She had the traits we needed to keep our pride strong and raise cubs we could be proud of. You can't imagine how many rivals I fought to get her. I didn't do it for love or attraction or whatever you wanna call it, I did it because she was right for the pride."

"Lily is right for the pride," Evan rebutted. "I don't love her. I've barely met her. Yeah, she's pretty to look at but so are half the women in Hollywood. She has the genes, I know it. That's the only reason I even mentioned her to you. Our pride needs to take her before another one does." He thrust his hands into his pockets and resumed pacing, distracted and irritated by memories of the woman's scent. His fingers brushed the car keys in his pocket, and the realization hit him. He still had Lily's cardigan in his car.

"I'm going downstairs. I'll be right back," he told his father and rushed out of the apartment.

The low, distant wail of sirens cast a bleak note over the darkened street. Evan wondered how his pride could stand living in downtown Los Angeles. Central City East was not the kind of place he liked coming home to. He had offered to help them relocate, but none had taken him up on the offer. There was too much blood of the pride in these streets, for better or worse. Evan remembered his own back-alley fights as a young, reckless cub. It was a wonder he was never caught. But then again, no one would believe a call to the police about lions running loose in LA.

He hated having to drive all the way out here, and though he had offered to discuss things with his father over steak dinner in Beverly Grove, the older man had insisted on staying home. Maybe it was for the better, as Evan needed to constantly remind himself to save money. Last night at the club he had been bleeding cash, but that too had been for the good of the pride. He had to make Lily his, no matter the cost.

Evan opened his car door and ducked into the back seat, feeling around for the soft fabric of Lily's sweater. The smell hit his nose instantly, and he knew it would be more than enough to convince his father. Sweater in hand, he delayed going back upstairs only long enough to send Lily a text asking her what she was doing tonight.

CHAPTER THREE

"Cut!" the director yelled. He tugged the faded baseball cap off his head and crushed it in his fist.

His wrinkled face showed Lily all she needed to know. She had been out of it all day, forgetting lines and awkwardly stumbling through her scenes. It wouldn't be the first time the director let her have it.

He pulled her aside. "You really want this, don't you?" he asked, putting a hand on his hip.

Lily felt like a child being scolded.

"I'm sorry," she replied. "I didn't sleep much last night."

In fact, she had been too busy worrying about the dark-colored sedan that kept cruising past her building. She had no doubt of who had been driving it. Though she had not seen the man in person since the night in the alleyway, his friends had been making their presence known. It seemed the man would not take no for an answer.

"Sweetheart, no one sleeps in this city. Your heart's not in it. And you were doing so well before. What changed?"

Sleeping with Evan, Lily thought. But that wasn't it. Her previous talent had just been beginner's luck. She was starting to lose what little confidence she had built in the last few days.

"I'm sorry," she apologized for the second time. "I'll shrug this off, whatever it is. I really do want to be here. I'll work harder."

"Let's wrap for today, and we'll make up the difference tomorrow. I'd rather give you a chance to get out of this funk than try to force your acting."

Lily nodded her thanks and let out a deep breath as soon as the director's back was turned. She walked off set towards a quieter part of the studio.

"You okay?" Evan asked, appearing beside her.

"You always ask me that," Lily replied.

"Well, are you?"

Lily rubbed her temple, where the start of a headache was forming. Evan reached around her shoulders and gave them a squeeze.

"That feels good," she said.

Evan's fingers continued to massage the tension out of her muscles as they talked.

"Whatever the director said to you, don't worry about it. You've been great so far.

Everyone has an off day once in a while. Do you want to go get something to eat?"

Lily shook her head. "No, I think I should go home early and rehearse. Maybe next time."

Evan looked disappointed. "You sure?"

"Yeah," Lily replied.

Evan shrugged and left for his trailer. Lily watched him go, but he didn't look back at her.

She and Evan had been seeing a lot of each other lately, both on set and off. He still kept that wall around him, the one guarding nearly everything about himself, but she was learning to ignore it. What they had was fun and would probably last through shooting, but Lily had a feeling that once the cameras stopped rolling, so too would their romance.

She had started to hear whispers on set about the two of them, her name being said in the same breath as a long list of Evan's past affairs. It seemed he was in the habit of drawing in a certain type of young, naïve actress and dropping them as soon as a new one came along.

But as long as Lily knew what she was in for, she didn't mind his reputation. She wasn't looking for anything long-term as she was still young and had a whole lifetime of meaningless romances ahead of her.

She opened the door to her trailer and let it slam behind her. The next thing she opened was the fridge, taking out the tube of cookie dough she had saved for such occasions. She plopped down onto the sofa, savoring the taste of butter and sugar as she balanced her script on one knee and flipped through it. Her lines, highlighted in pink, stood out on the page along with notes she had scribbled in the margins.

It was not a problem of memorizing lines, she told herself. That she could do with relatively little trouble. It was a problem of understanding the space of each scene, and her place in it. Her feeling of being lost in LA was starting to translate into her acting.

She felt unmoored, drifting between the glamour of Hollywood and the danger of central LA. Being cornered by the man in the alley had merely been the start. The next night, someone kept trying to buzz into her apartment building. The night after that, there was a single red rose in the elevator.

She hadn't thought it had any connection with what had happened, so she ignored it. The following night there was a full bouquet. When Lily read the card attached to it by a ribbon, she was shocked to find that it said, "To the brunette beauty with the dark blue eyes, until we meet again."

At first she thought it might have been Evan, but he would have just used her name. The night following the appearance of the bouquet, Lily was hassled on the street once again, this time by apparent friends of the man who had attacked her.

This time, though, they had kept their distance. Lily was starting to dread going home, tired of being harassed and not knowing what she would find when she got there. At least they did not know which apartment number was hers.

When Lily got to the end of the script, she closed it and tossed it onto the table. She still didn't feel confident, like there was some part of the character she was still missing. In thinking of what she could do to improve, she decided that she needed to get more acquainted with the set.

If she could stay late tonight, after everyone including the crew had left for the night, she would have the place to herself to rehearse. Though she didn't know if she technically had permission to do something like this, she knew it was important for her role. If she could become comfortable in that space, her acting would flow more naturally.

She stepped out of her trailer to have a look around. The studio was still quite busy so she gave up and went back inside. Almost as soon as she sat down, her eyes closed of their own volition. *A short rest,* she told herself, but when she awoke again it was already dark. She cursed herself for having fallen asleep.

She checked the clock on her phone. There was still enough time to rehearse. She fixed up her hair into a bun and wiped the sleep from her eyes, taking one last bite of cookie dough to fortify herself. If she wanted to be a star, she would have to put in the hours.

The studio building was almost foreboding, the cavernous space looking alien without all the cast and crew members milling about. No lights were on, except a single overhead floodlight in the main studio space left on for safety reasons. Lily stumbled through the semi-dark, searching for a light switch. She wasn't sure if she was even allowed on set after hours, but the thought did not concern her perhaps as much as it should have.

A metallic rattle, like something falling onto the floor, echoed through the space and Lily's breath caught in her throat. A badly-placed piece of equipment, she told herself. There was a low sound following it, almost like that of an animal. Lily's mind jumped to that night in the alley and the man who had attacked her, but she reassured herself the sound she had heard was only her own fear playing tricks.

Nevertheless, she waited a few moments before continuing towards the main set area. Her plan was to rehearse at least until she felt comfortable with the lines and had a feel for her character's headspace. The scene she had been struggling with that day had been one in which her character encountered a sudden shock, one that would change her relationship with the male protagonist in a profound way.

But she was having trouble separating Evan from his character, and found it hard to believe there was anything of substance beyond his handsome but two-dimensional surface.

The main set for the scene was built to look like the interior of the main protagonist's house. Walls could be pulled away and rearranged in order to get all of the necessary camera angles that would have been impossible inside a real house. Lily first went around the back, looking at the naked beams and planks of wood that made up the unfinished exterior of the set.

It was all so fake, she told herself. And while it was fun to play pretend, sometimes she just wanted something real.

Lily found the switch for the overhead lights on the far side of the main studio space and flicked them on, their sudden brilliance momentarily blinding her. When she opened her eyes again, there was a massive beast staring back at her from a catwalk underneath the row of lights. Its mane of golden hair shone brilliantly, but Lily's eyes were drawn more strongly to the beast's sharp teeth and massive claw-tipped paws.

She thought at first it was a prop, but when it blinked Lily realized it was real. It held her in its gaze as Lily stared back, too frightened to move. There was something almost alluring about its amber eyes.

Except in zoos, Lily had never seen a lion up close. She was as mesmerized as she was frightened. Sweat beaded on her skin as she stood in the hot halo of lamps, each droplet a brilliant diamond of reflected light. The animal, too, remained stock-still, only the powerful muscles of its hind legs twitching as if ready to pounce.

Lily wondered if it could jump the distance between the catwalk and herself without being injured, or if such a consideration would even cross the mind of such a regal beast. Surely it would jump without a second thought.

But even as Lily prepared for her last moments on earth, the lion turned around and slunk back into the darkness with the powerful grace that only wild animals possess. Either it was well-trained, or Lily did not look like a satisfying enough snack. Or maybe, it was just playing with its prey. Lily did not want to stick around to find out which.

But she also had to tell someone about it. The beast must have been an escapee from another project on the same lot. If it wasn't caught soon, others would be in danger.

There was a sound to Lily's right. Evan came running from seemingly nowhere, looking disheveled and breathing hard. His thin white t-shirt clung to his sweaty skin.

"You have to get out of here," he said.

"What are you doing here?" Lily asked. First the lion, and now Evan. Apparently, the set was not nearly as dead as she had thought.

Evan ignored her. "Go. I'll handle things."

Lily was hesitant to leave, and she hoped Evan would not do anything reckless. Even a man of his strength was no match for a lion. "Are you sure you're okay?" she asked.

"Yeah," Evan. "I'll close up the building then call 911. You should go home, or the cops will ask why you were here so late."

Evan's words confirmed Lily's suspicion that she may be trespassing and she became all the more eager to leave the studio.

She turned away from Evan, still wondering where he had come from, and walked briskly towards the exit. She fought her impulse to run, not knowing if lions were more apt to attack running prey. It seemed like a good idea to stay as inconspicuous as possible.

Feet from the exit, Lily broke into a run. She slammed the heavy metal door behind her and quick-walked all the way back to her car.

Once inside she let out a deep breath, taking a few moments to let the tension out of her system. Her hand shook as she tried to put the keys in the ignition. She gave up and threw the keys into the passenger seat. *What the hell was going on,* she thought. All she had wanted was a few quiet moments to herself to focus and practice the script, and she instead had found herself face to face with a fully-grown lion. Was the universe trying to tell her something?

Maybe she should have never come to LA. She was not meant for Hollywood. She was a small-town girl from Reno, Nevada. Not even Las Vegas. She had no place here, in this city of movie stars and big-name directors and live lions on the prowl after dark. Predators were closing in from all sides and she already had nowhere to run.

At least Evan had been there to take care of things, Lily thought. She was not sure what she would have done if he had not shown up. Probably panic and make things worse. She grabbed her keys off the passenger seat and turned on the car, her hands no longer shaking. The engine thankfully roared into life on her first try. Lily had to appreciate what small breaks the universe gave her.

* * *

There were few places he could risk shifting in the city, but a man with the literal heart of a lion could take those risks with little thought. Or so had been the case until Lily had shown up. Evan waited until her car disappeared into the city traffic before leaving himself.

Of course, he had no intention of calling the police, as he and the lion were one in the same. Why that woman had been on set so late was anyone's guess. Maybe she had fallen asleep in her trailer. But laziness was not a trait that the mates of alphas tended to possess. No, it was something else.

Evan drove westward through the Hollywood streets to his house in Beverly Grove. The neighborhood was good for young, single people who liked drinking and good food, and being near enough to the major studios was also a plus. It was amazing what one decent movie deal could achieve.

A year ago, he had still been scraping by in a cheap apartment down the block from his dad's, hauling himself around in the same used Pontiac that his older brother had bought in high school over a decade ago. His family was poor, to put it bluntly, and most of them still lived in the seedier parts of downtown LA. Evan had lost good friends to gang violence over the years and had witnessed a murder by the age of sixteen. Evan was not proud of his roots and did everything he could to bury them.

So, he had bought a nicer car and a bigger apartment. But some parts of himself couldn't be hidden by material purchases. At some point, he would have to tell Lily his secret, to explain what she had seen on set that night. It would scare her, but by then he hoped to have her so tightly in his grip that she would not be able to run away. There was nothing he could do about what had already happened, but he hoped his lie had been convincing enough to buy himself a little more time.

When Evan got back to his apartment, he bolted the door behind himself and pulled off his clothes. Before he had reached the back staircase leading to his private rooftop, he was already back in lion form. It was the only way he felt free from the petty human feelings of inadequacy and greed, of shame and fear.

Lions were not judged negatively on their fierceness, their desire to survive. That was exactly what Evan had done—survive. He had seen a way off the streets and had taken it. Though some members of his pride may have felt resentment at the way he now lived, the way he maintained a careful separation between his new life and his old one almost as if scared of contamination, Evan was just doing what was second nature to his species. Survive.

And Lily would help him do so. Evan paced the roof of his apartment building, trusting the cover of darkness to hide his animal form. Being around Lily was almost unbearable. The heat she gave off with every touch, every breath, threatened to crack the walls of Evan's control over his animal side and send them crumbling into dust.

His need to transform had more than doubled in intensity since that night at the club. And along with that animal lust came the aggression. It was a lot harder to work out of his system, and a lot deadlier. His biological pull towards her was telling him to protect his mate at all costs.

He soon gave up pacing and went back inside. There was somewhere he needed to be tonight, but he was stalling. He pulled on a dark pair of jeans and a leather jacket, and poured himself some whiskey to steel his nerves. The amber liquid burned on its way down, its comforting warmth settling deep down in his stomach.

Whiskey was something his father had taught him to love, the one indulgence his father would allow himself on an otherwise strict budget. Once, Evan recalled lifting a bottle of Four Roses from the liquor store for his dad's birthday. The reminder of his family gave Evan the kick he needed to force himself out the door.

The warmth was long gone by the time Evan made it to his destination. Matt was standing outside the dive bar in a paint-flecked grey hoodie, scuffing his worn sneakers against the pavement in a gesture that showed his nervousness all too well. Evan walked up to him and put an arm around his shoulder, not for brotherly camaraderie but rather for secrecy.

In a low voice, Evan said, "I only agreed to meet you here because I'm looking out for you. We only listen to what the guy has to say and we don't accept any of his money, okay?"

Matt pushed his brother away. The red in his cheeks told Evan he had already been drinking inside before Evan had shown up. "You don't have to treat me like your little brother. I'm older than you. I know what I'm doing."

"Just because you ran with them before, doesn't mean you have to go back. I'm taking care of your rent."

"Dad says you don't have enough."

"Screw the old man. He doesn't know what he's talking about. Now, can we go inside?"

In truth, Evan did need the money. But he was not going to start dealing drugs, and he was here to make sure his brother didn't fall back into it either. They were at the bar to meet with a member of the only other lion pride in their area, the one that had corrupted his brother all those years ago.

One of their members, a skeevy young guy named Al, had asked to meet Matt tonight to discuss a business opportunity. For whatever reason, Matt had been insistent on meeting Al, even though Evan had warned against it. Though his brother hated to admit it, Evan was there to protect him.

The inside of the bar was almost dangerously dark. A football game was on a grainy TV above the bar, the shouts of the those watching interjecting the din of clanking glasses and pool balls. The few, sticky tables were largely unoccupied. Most people either sat at the bar or stood around the pool tables in the back.

A couple made out by the door to the bathrooms. Matt held up two fingers to the bartender and was immediately handed two bottles of beer. Evan swigged his with reluctance, wanting the buzz but hating the old memories the sour taste brought back. The beer tasted of hot summers, of getting in fights with other cubs in the street and stealing alcohol from the backs of trucks parked outside of liquor stores.

It tasted of bad high school fumblings at love, when sex was an unobtainable dream and the steps leading up to it could only be described in bases. He hated who he had been then, and resented being forced to come back to all of it.

A man with a pool cue in hand nodded at Evan and Matt as they made their way through the bar towards him. Al was a thin man in his mid-twenties, with dark skin and longish hair. He had a long scar running down the side of his face, and Evan got flashes of the fight that had put it there. *Water under the bridge*, Evan tried to tell himself. Still his palms became sweaty as the man opened his mouth to greet them.

"Long time, no see, you stupid fucker," the man said with a cold smile. Whether deliberately or not, his hand went up to the crooked line on his face and he scratched at the taut skin.

Evan didn't bother to respond.

"He's not like that anymore," Matt said in his defense. "He does movies now."

The man looked surprised. "Well, if you're looking for actresses, I got a few girls who aren't too shy to show some skin."

Evan realized the man had the wrong idea. "Not that kind of movie," he replied.

Al looked disappointed. "Well, they're not good at memorizing lines so I guess they're no use to you."

"No, I guess not."

"It's too bad. There's a lot of money in that kind of work. And Matt says you're not making as much as you'd like to these days." Al bent down over the pool table as he talked. He squinted and lined up his shot.

Evan drank the last of his beer and set the bottle on the empty table behind him. He turned back around. "I'm in the middle of a project. I'll be fine."

"Then why are you here?"

"I'm looking out for Matt. He's the one who wanted to meet you."

"Looking out for your brother? But you haven't even paid his rent."

Hearing his father's words echoed in Al's voice set Evan on edge. Matt must have said something, the blabbermouth.

"I paid it today," he said loudly enough for Matt to hear. But his brother was nowhere to be seen.

"You paid half," Al said, sinking the 8-ball into the corner pocket. He immediately started gathering the balls up again to reset the game.

"What do you mean, I paid half?" Evan said.

"Rent doubled this month. Matt should have told you. The property market is crazy these days." The matter-of-fact way Al was saying this made Evan suspicious.

"Matt's renting from you guys, isn't he?" Evan said, his anger starting to bubble up from deep inside of him.

Al stepped back from the pool table and eyed his options. He glanced up at Evan. "Looks like you'll be needing that extra money now, doesn't it?"

"You can't con me into working for you."

"It's not a con. It's how things are."

There was a bitter taste in Evan's mouth, whether from the beer or the obvious lack of shame Al had in twisting the situation in his favor.

Al was leaning over the pool table again, focused on his game as if the situation with Evan was nothing but a passing distraction. Evan felt a burning desire to smash Al's face into the green velvet of the pool table.

He grabbed Al by the shoulder and pushed him up against the wall. The pool cue clattered to the floor as Evan put his face inches from Al's.

"Maybe you've forgotten who put that scar on your face, but I'd be happy to remind you." Though he had left this life behind, Evan found it almost too easy to slip back into it.

Al's face was a mask. He betrayed no emotions apart from the threat clear in his eyes. "As I recall, you have one or two yourself." His eyes flicked downwards momentarily.

Evan could feel the phantom pain of the thin scar running across his right side, where Al had tried to stab him when he'd turned his back during a fight. The man had no honor, fighting more like a snake than a lion.

Evan raised his fist, but Matt had raised the attention of the bartender and the two were already standing by in case things got ugly. Each man took one of Evan's arms and pulled him off Al before he could get a punch in.

"You and your friend need to leave," the bartender said sternly to Matt.

Matt held Evan roughly and pulled him out of the bar, dumping a wad of crumpled bills into the bartender's outstretched hand. Evan could hear Al's patronizing chuckle as they left the bar.

He was still fuming when they got outside. "Why didn't you tell me?" he shouted at his brother.

Matt faced him, his face showing equal parts rage with Evan's. "It was hard to find a place after I was locked up last time. One of the guys in Al's pride cut me a good deal."

"Why didn't you go back home?"

"I couldn't go back to living with Dad. It wasn't good for me or my wife, or our son. Dad's apartment's too small and we were fighting all the time. But you wouldn't know that because you'd already left us behind."

"That's not fair," Evan started.

But his brother was already halfway down the block. Evan knew there was something else he was hiding. It wasn't about the apartment, or the money. No honest man would run like that.

"You're using again," he shouted after his brother.

Matt stopped, but did not turn around. Evan caught up to him. "You're using again, I know it. It's not about the money. It's about the drugs. Al got you to relapse and now you're chained to him by your habit."

"You don't know what the fuck you're talking about," Matt spat. "I'd never go back."

He swung his fist, trying to hit his brother in the jaw. Evan ducked out of the way and caught Matt's wrist. He pulled Matt's sleeve up to his elbow, revealing the little red pinpricks hidden there.

Evan let go of his brother's wrist in disgust. "I thought so."

Matt pushed his sleeve back down. The fight had left his eyes. "Don't tell Kat, okay? I fucked up, but only once. Only 'cause I went to Al's to talk about why the rent was doubling and he had it all set up on the table in his living room. This fucking week. I was clean before that, I swear."

Evan could barely look at his brother. "Stay away from Al, and stay away from the heroin. Whatever his game is, we don't want to be a part of it. Can't you see he's trying to weaken our pride?"

"I promise, just please don't tell Kat. I don't know what I'd do if she left me."

Matt broke into a pathetic, drunken sobbing. Evan clapped him on the back a couple of times.

"I'm going to call a cab for you, okay?"

Matt nodded and sunk to the curb with his head in his hands. Evan stood off to the side, watching his brother with worry. For whatever reason, Al's pride was trying to corrupt Matt, so suddenly after so many years. Though the relationship between the two prides had always been volatile, this time they had crossed a serious line. If only Evan could find out why.

CHAPTER FOUR

The woman standing in Evan's trailer wore tight black jeans and boots up to mid-calf. Her dark hair was unnaturally straight, hanging low down her back and cut severely straight across the front. Her lips were a deep, almost black shade of blood red and her eye shadow was smoky and thick.

The pale yellow flower-print blouse she was wearing, set off by her dark skin, was the only thing gentle about her. She had apparently stolen it off Lily's costume rack. It still held Lily's irresistible scent, and Evan did all he could to resist it.

He pointed at the door with a hard look. "You need to leave."

The woman pouted. "I thought you'd be happy to see me. It's been too long."

"Why now, all of a sudden?" Evan asked.

The last time he had seen Jade she had called him a pig and slammed a door in his face. Their romance had been one of constant fighting and inescapable chemistry. And like any poison, it had almost killed him.

"I saw your picture in a magazine and Al was kind enough to tell me where you're working," she said, moving towards him.

He backed up.

"So, I'm not a pig anymore?"

Jade laughed, the crystal-clear tones sounding harsh to Evan's ears. The woman's obvious attraction to fame repulsed him, but her stolen smell was driving him wild.

"No," she purred. "You're not. I'm flattered you remember my words so well."

She placed her hand on his chest and drove him backwards. Evan fell down onto the sofa and she straddled him before he could get back up.

Evan was paralyzed by the strength of Lily's smell on the blouse. He wanted to push her away but he could not.

Jade pinched the fabric to her nose and took a deep breath. "It's amazing what you can find out just hanging around a movie set for an hour. I didn't know you had a girlfriend."

"That's not yours. Take it off."

She started to lift the edge of the blouse. "Are you sure?"

Evan stopped her hand. "She's not my girlfriend. And neither are you, anymore." He struggled to keep his voice even.

She caressed his cheek with her hand and then slid her fingers through his hair. Her face was inches from his. "Does she know what you are?" she asked. Her hot breath pressed against Evan's skin.

"What if she does?" Evan replied.

Jade took Evan's hand and guided it up the curve of her body. She ground against him as if giving him a lap dance.

"She won't accept you," she breathed, her words cutting like a knife. "She's not one of us. I have everything you're looking for. I can give you strong cubs. I know she has the scent, but just by looking at me you can see who has the stronger genes."

Evan pulled his hand away, gritting his teeth in resolve. "If your genes are so strong, why were you kicked out of your own pride?"

Jade hissed and pushed herself away from Evan. He breathed in a lungful of air to try and clear out the unwanted lust burning in his chest.

"They were weak. Stupid," she shouted. Her face was a mask of rage.

Evan had hit a sensitive spot. Jade's pride no longer lived in Los Angeles. Years ago, they had kicked her out and left the city, abandoning her to the streets and a life of trying to be accepted into another pride.

So far it hadn't worked. Jade was rotten and all the prides knew it. She would have been better off moving to another city and starting over.

Evan stood. He was slowly regaining his control. "I'm not getting back together with you. If you're so desperate to join a pride, you might try lowering your standards."

Jade shot him a disgusted look, which morphed into a twisted smile as she moved towards the door. "Maybe I will," she replied. "But don't think that girl's yours. You can't keep a secret like her all to yourself. The other lions will be on her soon enough."

Evan made another gesture towards the door and this time Jade obeyed. Evan was glad to see the back of her. No good things could come from her reentering his life.

* * *

Last night, Lily had dreamed of lions. She had dreamed of being stalked in the tall grass by one with golden fur and another of a darker, dustier hue. The golden lion had made her feel almost excited, like her heart was about to burst out of her chest. There was something alluring in its danger. But the darker lion had brought only fear. Lily had escaped them in her dream, only to find herself lost in the streets of LA.

By then, the golden lion had gone, leaving only the darker lion to pursue her. Traffic filled the streets and Lily wove between the stopped cars, never able to move fast enough to ease her fear and the sense that the hunter was gaining on her. In the end, her alarm woke her before he could pounce.

Her dream came back in pieces as she walked through the bustling set. A man carrying a half-dressed mannequin passed her, followed by two more trailing wagons of sound equipment. She waved at the last man, recognizing him as part of her film's crew. He smiled and nodded, unable to free his hands to wave.

The person Lily really wanted to see this morning was Evan, but he was nowhere to be found. She wanted to know that he was okay, and that the lion situation had been taken care of.

But most of all, Lily needed to know she wasn't crazy. When she had first gotten on set that morning, she thought she had seen him but he had quickly disappeared into a storage closet so it must not have been him after all.

When she had told Tessa of encountering the lion, her best friend had not seemed nearly as shocked. In fact, Tessa was adjusting to living in LA quite well and nothing about this crazy, sprawling city seemed to phase her. Though Lily was glad for her friend's ability to adjust, she was also envious.

Lily was still trying to find her feet in so many ways.

Lily drifted around set asking anyone who would listen if they knew what had happened to the loose lion the night before. No one seemed to have any idea what she was talking about.

"Really, you haven't heard anything?" Lily asked one of the makeup crew. She almost added that she had seen the beast with her own eyes, but caught herself just in time.

The woman dusted Lily's cheeks with blush. "Sorry, no clue. Where did you say you heard about it from?"

"Um, I thought I heard some people talking about it outside the studio this morning," she said after the woman finished with the blush. "But never mind. I must have been mistaken."

The makeup woman shrugged and continued with her work.

A slightly older woman slid into the unoccupied seat next to Lily's and one of the artists swooped in to tend to her makeup. "You're the one asking about the lion," the actress said as she watched her own reflection in the mirror.

"Yeah," Lily replied. "Have you heard about it?"

The woman's eyes wrinkled at the corners, but her lips betrayed only the hint of a smile. "I might have. You're not the first young actress whose imagination's run away from her after a long day on set. Somehow, it's always lions that they see. Maybe it's the associations with show business, that one company's logo. Was anyone else there when you thought you saw the lion?"

"No," Lily said. She didn't want to feed further into the on-set rumors about her relationship with her costar.

"I thought so," the woman replied with an almost smug look on her face. "By the way, I heard you're spending a lot of time with Evan McKay."

Lily was starting to not like this woman and her self-satisfied way of talking. "Maybe," Lily said with a little too much defensiveness in her voice.

The woman tutted. "All you girls are the same. I'd be careful if I were you. He doesn't keep his promises, and you wouldn't be the first to throw away your potential chasing after him. Even now you're probably not the only one he's seeing. LA's full of good men. You should try to find one of them instead. That is, after you've grown up a little. Good men don't go for the naïve ones."

Lily's desire to find Evan returned in full force. She wanted to be saved from having to listen to any more of this bitter old woman's words. Also, she knew she would not be able to work until she heard the resolution to last night's excitement, and on top of that she found it strange that no one had even heard of the incident. Almost suspicious. She stood up from her makeup chair, startling the woman tending to her.

"Where are you going? You're not done yet," the woman called after Lily, who was already hurrying across the studio lot to the actors' trailers.

A woman was leaving Evan's trailer just as Lily approached. She was tall, curvy, and possessed a swagger that Lily envied. Her long hair was mussed and she ran a finger through it to comb it out. Lily noticed that her blouse looked familiar, but she couldn't quite place it. Maybe Tessa had the same one.

She winked at Lily as they passed each other. Lily only stared as she puzzled over the woman's business in Evan's trailer and the meaning behind her wink.

Lily tried to put the mystery woman out of her mind as she knocked on Evan's door. Evan opened it, his wavy hair hanging low over his brow. He looked surprised to see her, and if she wasn't mistaken, a bit uneasy.

"Sorry, did I bother you?" she asked, thinking back to the woman.

"Actually, I've got some things to do," Evan said, seeming nothing like his usual self. There was none of that aggressiveness. He wasn't chasing her, nor trying to draw her towards him. If anything, he was trying to push her away.

He nearly shut the door on her, but Lily spoke up before he could. "I just wanted to ask what happened with the lion last night. No one else on set seems to have even heard about it. Do those kinds of things not even make the news in LA?"

"I guess not," Evan replied, looking like he wanted the conversation to be over with. He moved to close the door again.

"But you called the police, right? Did they find out where the lion came from? What happened to it?" Lily could tell that Evan was not in the mood to talk, but her questions came tumbling out of her. She couldn't shake the feeling that something was off.

Evan sighed heavily and leaned out the doorway. "Okay, fine. Come in here." He stepped back from the door to give Lily room to enter.

The door shut behind her with a rattle.

There she was, standing in his trailer, about to find out something that very few people knew about him. And all he could think about was devouring her. After Jade's tease, though, he had no interest in her specifically, Evan had only one thing on his mind.
He could see the full shape of Lily's breasts as her thin t-shirt clung to them, the fabric doing Evan no favors to help him control his desire.

"By the way, who was that woman?" Lily asked, adding yet another unanswerable question to the growing pile.

"She was my agent," Evan lied, using the first thing that popped into his mind.

Lily responded to his answer with a frown whose meaning Evan could not piece out.

"So, are you going to tell me what happened last night?" Lily asked, moving her hands to her hips. The pose only further emphasized the swell of her breasts.

Evan shook his head. He debated distracting her from her line of questioning by kissing her instead, but he knew that sooner or later he would have to tell her if he wanted her to be his mate. He decided to get it over with.

"I have to show you something," he said and started pulling his shirt over his head.

Lily looked alarmed. "Really? Now? I'm supposed to be shooting a scene in fifteen minutes."

Evan tossed his shirt onto the ground and said, "I'm not trying to start anything. I swear. But I need to take my clothes off. You'll understand soon."

Lily rolled her eyes when she thought Evan wasn't looking. Evan could have chuckled had the situation not been so serious for him at the moment. Lily was slowly, but surely, starting to gain the confidence she needed to really shine as an actress. Evan liked to think he had something to do with that.

Evan stood naked in front of Lily, feeling suddenly self-conscious though she had seen his body before. Instead, he focused on his transformation, allowing the animal to flow out from his center until it overcame his human nature. He was barely aware of the physical changes, the coarse fur sprouting across his body and the rippling growth of his muscles. He was instead preoccupied with the growing awareness of Lily's irresistible scent and lust boiling within him.

Lily's eyes widened and her hands flew to her mouth. It seemed she was doing all she could not to scream. Evan stood stock still, not wanting to startle her into any adverse reaction. He held her gaze as he had the night before. *It's me,* he thought, as if trying to transmit his thoughts to her through his eyes. *I'm not going to hurt you.*

As Evan waited for Lily's response, he felt himself growing almost intoxicated with her smell. It had also been strong last night, but then he had been on a catwalk yards away from her. In the cramped quarters of his actor's trailer, there was nowhere for the scent to go but straight into his nostrils.

"Okay, okay. This is some kind of a trick, right?" Lily mumbled. "I mean, you're not really, you can't really, oh god."

Evan took a step towards her, and Lily instinctively retreated back against the wall. "Hey, whoa," she called out, her voice wobbling.

He was having a hard time controlling his instincts. He took another step forward, then another. He wanted more of her scent. When there was nowhere left for her to run, he pounced, standing on his hind legs and landing his forepaws on the wall on either side of her.

At full height, he towered over Lily, his head nearly hitting the ceiling of the trailer.
Lily stood stock still, as if scared to even breathe. Evan wanted to taste her, to devour her. He struggled with his own impulses, the man and animal grappling inside of him for command over his body.

He leaned down low, the end of his snout grazing the top of Lily's head. His breath puffed against her dark hair. It would be all too easy to fit her inside his jaws. After a tense minute, he lowered himself back onto the floor and forced himself to shift back.

Lily came to him nervously as he crouched on all-fours. panting from the effort of bottling up his power. She slipped a gentle, slightly shaking arm around his heaving shoulders.

"What are you?" she asked.

"We're called shifters," Evan replied. He stood with some effort and started dressing. Lily watched him closely. "You caught me last night at a bad time. I didn't think anyone would be around."

Lily looked a little pale. Evan had her sit down.

He said, "I'm not the only one. There are whole prides of us, all over LA and other cities too. We can shift at will, but it takes a lot of control to be able to do so."

"So, it's not a magic trick?" Lily asked.

"No," Evan said, though he knew Lily's question was rhetorical. "No one else knows about this, outside of a select few people. I'm counting on you not to tell anyone."

Lily stared wide-eyed at Evan and he could only guess his words were getting through to her.

"I mean no one," he repeated.

Lily slowly nodded.

"I'm not trying to scare you," Evan continued. "But I'm sure you can imagine the danger if something like this gets out."

"It's okay," Lily said. "I won't tell anyone. I promise."

"Good," Evan replied. "I mean, I know you won't. I trust you."

Lily tried to hide her smile at these words but Evan caught it. Her face was flushed red. She stood. "I—I should get back to set. I'm supposed to be filming a scene now."

Evan leaned down and kissed her on the forehead, a gesture that he hoped would seal her promise. He could not tell how the exposure of his secret would affect their relationship long-term, as he had never told someone like this. He would just have to wait and see.

CHAPTER FIVE

"I think that guy's a neighbor of ours. I keep seeing him around the building." Tessa nodded over Lily's left shoulder, indicating to a man in a baseball cap across the café from where they sat.

Lily tried to get a good look at him without seeming suspicious. She glanced at the man then up at the wall clock behind him. She didn't recognize him. He was wearing a baseball cap low over his face and he looked old compared to the groups of young people typing away on their laptops and phones around him. His gut hit the edge of the table where he sat.

"Sorry, I don't recognize him," Lily said as she turned back around.

"Are you sure?" Tessa asked. "You must have seen him before. He's always wearing that same Dodgers cap."

"Nope."

Lily put her coffee to her lips and winced at the burning liquid. She put the cup back down and popped off the lid to let it cool.

Tessa frowned. "I swear you've seen him. He's around a lot in the evening."

"Probably that's when he gets off work and goes home," Lily replied. "Besides, I haven't exactly been coming home every night."

Tessa gave Lily a sly smile. "Oh yeah, how are things with Mr. Bigshot McKay?"

Lily still had not told Tessa about Evan being a shifter. She had been weighing the pros and cons in her head, and could still not come to a confident decision. "Good," she replied lamely.

"Are you guys like, dating, now?"

Lily inhaled some of her coffee. She sputtered and put down her cup. "No, we just hooked up once," she choked. "No one on set seems to be taking it seriously, so I'm not either. I mean, if it becomes something I'm not exactly going to stop it but I'm not holding my breath either."

Tessa's voice took on a suspicious tone. "Okay, whatever you say. I'm only wondering when I should be expecting him for dinner."

"Even if we were dating, I'd never take him back to our dump," Lily retorted. She could not imagine a guy like Evan sitting at her dismal kitchen table, with the sounds of weekend partiers outside and the smell of the restaurant next door wafting in through their poorly insulated windows.

"Scoot your chair around to my side," Tessa said, leaning in conspiratorially. "I want you to watch him with me."

"Who?" Lily asked.

"The guy who might be our neighbor."

"Why?" The man didn't seem to be bothering anyone, and she didn't want to look like a creep staring at him.

Tessa shrugged. "It's just a hunch. Don't worry, I'll pull out my phone so it just looks like we're going over selfies together. If he keeps looking at us, we'll know something's up."

Lily rolled her eyes. "Or maybe he's weirded out by the crazy blond woman who keeps staring at him. It's only natural he'd come to the same coffee shop as us, considering our apartment's only a few blocks away. He probably lives in one of the buildings around here, that's all."

Tessa ran a self-conscious hand through her hair. "I'm telling you. I didn't see him until a few days ago, but now he's everywhere. I see him more than those thugs who keep harassing you."

Lily had almost forgotten about them, as they had not been around to bother her lately. In fact, things had been strangely quiet.

"I'm sorry," Tessa said. "That whole thing was really scary for you. I'm glad they're gone."

"Don't worry about it," Lily mumbled with her coffee cup in front of her mouth.

She turned over her shoulder to glance back at the man in the Dodgers cap, purely out of curiosity. He was reading a newspaper and generally minding his own business. The bell on top of the front door tinkled as it opened and the man looked up. He quickly folded his newspaper, pulled his cap lower on his head, and headed out the side door.

Lily turned to see who might have spooked him, and upon looking towards the door she was shocked. The man who had just entered the café was none other than the man who had cornered her in the alley. Today he was wearing a bright summery shirt and sunglasses, but his features were unmistakable.

Lily turned back around to Tessa. "Hey, let's get out of here," she said.

"Why?" Tessa asked. "I haven't even finished my latte."

Lily's palms were sweating. She needed to get out of there. "It's the guy," she muttered under her breath, not wanting to draw attention to herself. "The one that attacked me."

Tessa looked over. "You mean the good-looking guy who just walked in here? With the sunglasses?"

Lily did not bother to take another look. "Yes, now can we go?"

"Shouldn't we call the cops or something?"

"It happened a week ago, and I don't have any proof it was him. The cops didn't help me that night, so why would they now?"

"Okay, okay," Tessa replied, looking concerned. She stood up and, blocking the man's view of Lily as best she could, led her friend out the same door the man in the Dodgers cap had used.

Once outside, Lily felt like she could breathe again. She started walking down the street back towards the apartment and Tessa followed.

"That was him?" she asked.

"Yeah." Lily didn't feel like talking about it. She just wanted to forget that man's face.

Tessa seemed to pick up on this. "Hey," she said, her voice perking up, "Let's go do some shopping. It won't do you any good to mope around the apartment all day." She hooked her arm around Lily's and started walking with purpose in the other direction.

Lily had no choice but to turn and follow her, or risk toppling over altogether. Though she wanted to go home and hide under her covers, she knew that it would not be good for her overall emotional health to do so. She trusted that the shopping trip with Tessa would lift her spirits.

They hopped on the metro and took it into Hollywood, Tessa spending most of the trip on her phone with a client. Lily didn't mind that her friend was busy, as it gave Lily a chance to sort through her own thoughts, which had been piling up faster than she could deal with them.

First, there was the situation with Evan. Even without finding out that he was some sort of shape shifting lion man, things had been complicated enough. Lily couldn't be completely sure that the woman she had seen coming out of his trailer had been his agent. There was something about her slightly disheveled appearance that had made Lily suspicious.

Not that she and Evan were exclusive, but it seemed kind of crass to go about things in such an obvious way. Maybe that night at the lookout had not been as mind-blowing as Lily remembered, and Evan had already started to lose interest. Lily had to be prepared for the possibility that she would never get closer to Evan than she was now. Even after sharing his secret with her, he was still just another Hollywood playboy. He could leave at any time.

At the same time, there was the problem of the assault and men who had been following her since then. She was not ready to believe that the man Tessa had singled out in the Dodgers cap had anything to do with those men, but seeing the man who had attacked her at the café had sent Lily into alert mode.

She no longer felt comfortable in her neighborhood, and promised herself she would not walk there alone after dark. Whether that meant waiting late for Tessa to come home or taking a cab directly to the front door of her apartment building, she would not let herself be vulnerable again. Those men clearly meant trouble.

They arrived at their station, pulling Lily out of her troubling thoughts. Tessa dragged Lily all over Hollywood, from upscale boutiques to kitschy tourist traps. She was like a child in a candy store. Everything caught her eye and made her want it. Though she walked away with few actual purchases, whether it was a pale blue sun dress or an off-brand replication of some celebrity's Oscar gown, Tessa just had to try it on.

Lily had almost as much fun watching her friend as Tessa had wearing each outfit. Lily herself had little interest in trying on new clothes, as much of her job entailed just that. Wardrobe always seemed to be searching for the next perfect outfit to make her glow onscreen. She was about ready to tell them to give it up, as she would never be the glamorous star they wanted her to be.

After a whirlwind of window shopping and a lunch of seafood and cocktails at a place called The Hungry Cat, Lily was feeling a lot better. She didn't even mind when, about mid-afternoon, Tessa had to leave to meet with a client.

"Sorry, Lil. I'll catch you for dinner. Text me where you want to go."

"Sure thing."

Tessa straightened her purse strap on her shoulder and gave her friend a wave goodbye.

Lily, having had her fill of Hollywood for the day, decided to take the train back to Koreatown and spend the afternoon lazing around the apartment and maybe doing some light cleaning. She waited on the above ground platform of the nearest train station, enjoying the warm sunshine and watching the weekend crowd of young people and families, both tourists and locals, go about their business.

The train came and its doors slid silently open. As Lily stepped on, she chanced to look to her right and saw a tall man in a brightly colored shirt and sunglasses stepping into the train a couple of cars down. Before she could register what was happening, the doors had already shut behind her. Had he followed her here from Koreatown, and had he been trailing her all day?

She was trapped on the train with the man from the alley, and there was nowhere to go until the next stop. Lily nervously moved to the back of the car, farthest from the one the man had entered and waited by the door. Her breath came out in nervous pants as she struggled to keep it under control.

The announcement for the next station came on and the train slowed to a stop. It seemed an agonizingly long time before the car doors opened enough for Lily to slip through. Standing on the platform, she stared at the open doors of the car to her left in fear. She could see a little ways into the train, the seats largely occupied but no one looking to get off. Lily breathed a sigh of relief.

But then the man stepped off, seemingly out of nowhere. Lily turned to get back on the train but the doors were already shut and the train was pulling out of the station. Lily started walking quickly towards the exits. Her pumps clacked too loudly on the cement, and she stumbled getting on the escalator. She did not know if the man was following her, but she did not want to look back.

She hurried up the escalator and outside, running straight into a chaotic crowd of tourists. They were probably on their way to Madame Tussauds and the Walk of Fame. A woman waving a flag was trying to round up the mass of people with cameras hanging around their necks and pink faces from the LA sunshine.

Lily thought maybe she could lose the man in the crowd, but she could not make any progress through the tightly-packed crowd.

She felt a hand close on her upper arm as the man's body loomed over hers. She tried to get away but the people in front of her would not budge.

"Stop, I just want to talk." His silky voice slipped into her ear under the commotion of the crowd. Lily tried to pull her arm away, but he held on tightly. "I was drunk, and I scared you. Let me apologize."

Lily did not believe a word out of his mouth. She wanted to get away, but he was firmly pushing her towards the edge of the crowd. She could feel his chest against her shoulder and smell his aftershave. "Let me go," she demanded.

He looked down at her, his dark eyes almost apologetic, but said nothing as he continued to herd her away from the station. Lily decided that he could not keep hold of her forever, and when the opportunity presented itself she would escape. At least this time, it was midday and she was in a crowded part of Hollywood so he could not try anything untoward without being caught immediately.

When they were far enough down the street, the man showed her into a tiny restaurant that would have been easy to miss had Lily not been forced to go there. The air was thick with hookah smoke and the sharp smell of spices filled the air. A couple of older men and a younger woman who looked like she could have been one of their daughters shared a table in the corner. They barely looked up when Lily entered. Seeing another woman there made Lily feel safer.

The man caught her off-guard by pulling her chair out for her and she sat down without thinking. When she tried to stand again, the man held out his hand to stop her.

"Please, give me five minutes. We'll both feel better if you let me apologize."

Though Lily did not trust the man, she found herself staying in her seat. His gaze held hers as she made the decision not to leave just yet.

A waiter came by with a pot of tea and a small plate of confections Lily did not recognize and set them on the table. The man across from her ignored them.

"Did you get the flowers?" he asked.

"No," she lied. Had those roses been his pathetic attempt at an apology?

"My friends told me what I did, that night. I barely even remember. I was so drunk, and I tend to get nasty when I drink. You made me crazy. I couldn't help it."

Lily's stomach knotted with revulsion. The way the man's words echoed those of Evan's the night they first hooked up made Lily want to scream.

The man put his hands palm-up on the table, as if showing her he was hiding no foul intentions in their grip. "I've told my friends to stop harassing you. I want a fresh start. I want to take you out to dinner sometime. Maybe drinks. My name's Darien and yours is Lily, and I think we will get along very well."

It may have been the handsomeness of his features, or his almost dangerous confidence in the way he said her name, but for a moment

Lily was nearly lured in by his charm. She briefly imagined the feel of his jet-black beard against her skin.

Lily shook the vision from her head and stood up. "I can't accept your apology and I won't forget what you did. If I see you again I'm calling the police."

With that, Lily turned and left the restaurant. She walked back toward the station. Darien was nowhere to be seen, but still Lily could not shake the feeling she was being followed. There was something sinister about Darien's apology, like it was another calculated attempt to lure Lily into his trap. She decided to wait a while before going back to her apartment, as she had a bad feeling of what might be waiting for her when she got there.

When the lights finally started to fade over the Hollywood hills, Lily was reminded of the sunrise she had missed all those nights ago, while Evan held her in his arms. In that moment there had been, as there always was, a feeling of connection that had made Lily feel like maybe there was something more. But since then, their relationship had been mostly physical. Evan was still not willing to break down that wall of his around his life for her.

Lily was starting to feel hungry, and gave Tessa a call. Her friend picked up on the last ring before voicemail.

"Sorry, Lil," she said immediately upon picking up. "I'm going to be late with my client. I don't have time to go out, but if you want I can bring something back to the apartment when I finish."

"No, it's fine," Lily replied. "I don't want you to feel like you have to hurry home. I'll pick up something myself." She started wandering towards the station.

"I'll make it up to you tomorrow, okay?"

Lily agreed and hung up. Now that Tessa was not joining her for dinner, Lily was even more reluctant to head back towards her apartment. By the time she got to her station, it would be dark and those six blocks from the station to her house would be dangerous, and not only because of Darien and his friends. A lone woman in the city had to be wary of these kinds of things.

Keeping her phone out, she called Evan next. He was the only person she could think of. After all, he was a lion. If there was anyone qualified to keep her safe on the streets of Los Angeles, it was Evan. Though they weren't really in enough of a relationship to warrant her asking him to help her home like this, she had to try. Either that or waste money on a cab from her station. If she was lucky, he'd be somewhere he could pick her up from Hollywood.

His deep voice came in after only a couple of rings. "Yeah?"

95

"It's Lily."

"Oh, hey." The TV was on in the background. Baseball, from the sound of it.

"Are you busy?"

"Not really."

Lily debated asking him to dinner first, but she knew it would become a whole thing and wasn't feeling up for it. "Where are you now?"

"Um..."

There was a pause, as if Evan either was not sure how to respond or he didn't want to. Lily wondered if he was with another woman. But if that was the case, why could she hear a baseball game in the background?

Finally, Evan answered, "I'm near downtown. Why?"

Lily started heading toward the station, knowing that Koreatown lay between where she was in Hollywood and downtown. If she asked Evan to pick her up here, he would have to backtrack to drop her off at her apartment. She didn't want to make things any more inconvenient for him if she could help it.

"It's kind of a long story, but I was wondering if you could give me a ride to my apartment from the station. It's only a few blocks, but there's been some incidents in the neighborhood recently and I don't feel safe on my own. Sorry. I don't really know anyone else to ask."

The tone of Evan's voice was hard to decipher. He did not sound particularly reluctant, but there was a distance to it that Lily realized she had not been expecting. "Yeah sure. Which station?"

"Wiltshire/Vermont."

"Okay, give me half an hour. I'll meet you inside the station."

"Thanks," Lily managed before Evan hung up.

It was the second time that day that a McKay had been to Koreatown. Evan couldn't believe that his father had come here several times throughout the week looking for Lily, but Evan knew that the old man wouldn't have been able to rest until he saw for himself the woman who Evan had chosen to be his mate. And he was glad his father had, because now they knew they were not the only lions stalking Lily.

His father's visit to the coffee shop Lily and her friend had been chatting at had been cut short by the arrival of a man from Al's pride who was next in line for dominance. His name was Darien and he already had a reputation in the city for both his cunning and brutal good looks. Already the combination of the two had gotten him far in the underground economy of the city, and it was just a matter of time before he challenged for the position of alpha within his pride.

When that time came, Evan knew his own pride's days would be numbered. Darien, much like Evan, possessed ambitions that the rest of his pride did not, and these ambitions did not leave any room for competition. But unlike Evan, Darien ran a cartel and was not above using unsavory means to achieve his ends.

Which is why his appearance at the same coffee shop as Lily that morning had worried Evan. There was no way the man could have been so close to her without picking up her scent. Maybe he had not been able to pinpoint the source, but knowing that such a mate was out there was enough.

Darien would likely now be stalking the city looking for Lily with the intent to make her his mate. This was part of the reason Evan had agreed to walk her home tonight. He couldn't run the risk of any other lions getting to her.

When Evan got to Lily's station, she was already waiting for him. Though her clothes were casual and her hair tied up messily, she still looked stunning, even in the harsh overhead lights of the station's platform.

"Hey," he nodded, walking up to her. Seeing her face light up as he approached gave him a warm feeling in his chest. *Satisfaction, not affection*, he told himself. She was that much closer to being his.

"I don't have my car, so we'll have to walk," he said.

"It's no problem. Thanks for coming all the way out here."

As they turned to leave the station, he softly put his hand on Lily's back. He smiled to himself as she leaned into his touch. *He should probably invite himself in*, he thought hoping her roommate was not going to be home.

Lily turned south as they left the soft halo of lights around the station.

"Don't tell me your apartment's this way," Evan said as he followed her. He had a very bad feeling about where they were going.

Lily shrugged. "I didn't know anything about the city when I first got here. I guess I should have done some more research. I know it's dangerous, but that's why you're walking me home."

Dangerous, and the home of Darien's pride. Whereas most of Evan's pride lived in central LA near downtown, Darien's pride had holed itself up in the seedy parts of south Koreatown. Here they could get away with almost anything. Down here was like a time capsule of Hollywood thirty years ago, where drugs and prostitution flourished in the shadows just underneath the marquees of theaters and upscale hotels.

Cleaning out "tinsel town" had pushed most illegal activities down here, right into the lap of the lions who had no objections profiting from it. Lily, with her pheromones' irresistible pull drawing the lions to her, could not have chosen a worse place to live in the entire city.

As they walked further into the territory of his rivals, Evan put his arm protectively around Lily's shoulder, shielding her from the invisible threat he felt around them. His eyes darted back and forth across the street.

"When you called me, you said there were some incidents around here. What happened?"

Lily's steps faltered a little, as if startled by the question.

"Assaults, harassment, that kind of thing. Nothing serious like a murder, but I'd rather not take my chances."

"Have you been bothered by anyone?" Evan asked.

Lily's voice caught in her throat. "I—"

A car passing by honked loudly, cutting off Lily's thought. It swerved between lanes, its angry red taillights eventually disappearing as it took the turn at a stop sign without even slowing down.

The street became still again once the car was out of sight but Lily too had fallen silent.
Evan did not feel comfortable asking again. Though she knew about his secret, he did not want to invite the closeness that such a conversation would entail. They walked the rest of the way to her apartment in silence.

"This is me," she said in front of rather anemic looking building stacked next to a noodle shop.

The smell of red pepper and broth was strong. The paint on the front of the apartment building was crumbling and flaking off, and the nameplates on the buzzer for the front door were covered over in yellowing paper labels. Lily's name was not on any of them, and Evan suspected that the landlord had not changed them in ages.

"Do you want me to walk you up?" Evan asked with a half-smile.

He could sense Lily's embarrassment at where she lived, but he also wanted very much to be invited into her apartment. Ever since the night in his car, he had been trying to catch her again but they had never managed more than a quick make-out in a quiet corner of the set. The constant tease was almost worse than nothing at all.

"No, it's okay," Lily replied. "Tessa's probably home anyway."

"What floor?" Evan asked.

"Third."

Evan glanced up at the building. All the lights on the third floor were out. Unless there were rooms that faced to the other side of the block that Evan couldn't see, there was a good chance Lily's roommate wasn't home.

"I'll take my chances," he said.

Lily gave a shy smile and let him into the building.

CHAPTER SIX

It was nearing midnight when Evan finally left Lily's apartment. He had debated staying until morning, but by then Tessa had come home and the apartment had started to feel quite small. It was not that Evan had anything against Lily's roommate, but he did not want to seem too familiar too soon. If he became something akin to a boyfriend to Lily, things would become predictable, boring.

The sexual tension currently keeping them chasing after each other was exciting. It was nebulous and charged with energy, the pure physical attraction pulling them to each other like magnets.

As Evan stepped onto the now quiet street, he became aware of a familiar smell. It was not Lily's perfume still clinging to his skin, but rather a foul, feral note that rose Evan's hackles.

The very man Evan did not want to see anywhere near Lily stepped out of the shadows by the entrance to Lily's apartment followed by two other thugs whose names Evan could not recall. They slowly approached him as if they had been waiting for him all this time. Darien had his hands in his pockets, a knowing smirk on his face.

"So you've found her too," he said, coming nearer. The two other men kept a step or two behind, an unconscious display of obedience.

As far as they were concerned, Darien was already the alpha. "I thought I saw your old man stalking her this morning, but it's good to have confirmation. I wondered how long it would take for you bastards catch her scent."

Realization sunk like a stone in Evan's gut. He was not the only one after Lily. He should have known. He shouldn't have been so cocky.

Darien stalked closer. "You stink of her. What have the two of you been up to?"

Evan took a step forward to meet his challenger. He could not show weakness. "I've already claimed her. She's mine. You and your men need to stay the hell away."

"Or what?" Darien asked.

"Or it's war, and you don't want that."

Darien chuckled. "Don't think you're the only one who's allowed to taste just how sweet she is. She may not even want you when we're done."

Evan could not tell if he was bluffing, but it didn't matter. Lily was his. He snarled and pushed Darien up against the side of the building. Darien's two companions were quick to pull Evan off before he could do much more than ruffle Darien's shirt. He struggled out of their grip and stood panting on the pavement, seeing only red.

"You piece of shit," he spat.

Darien kept his calm, despite Evan's visible aggression. He said, "You have no claim on her. Not yet, anyway."

"She'll never be yours," Evan growled, trying to rein in his bloodlust. He could not give in to the violence raging in his veins. He could not go back to his old self. He had to maintain his human control.

"We both want the same mate, and one of us is going to have to yield. Either we keep playing this game or we fight and decide it once and for all."

Evan lunged at Darien, furious that the man thought he had any sort of claim on Lily. Though he refused to dignify Darien's challenge with a formal fight, he was not above getting in a few punches while he could.

Evan was vaguely aware of the other two shifters running off. It seemed their loyalty to their new alpha was not so cemented as

Darien might have liked. Evan was glad to see them leave. This fight was between him and Darien, no one else.

As he turned to watch them, Darien's fist made contact with Evan's temple, the ring on his middle finger cutting deep. Blood ran down Evan's forehead and into the corner of his eye, temporarily blurring his vision. He shook his head in rage. The urge to shift was burning him up inside, but he had to keep it under control. As dead as the street was at this hour, this was no place to shift. Eyes could be watching from any number of windows facing the street, and it only took one to make a call to the police.

Darien swung again and missed as Evan stumbled, dazed from the last blow, his momentum sending him reeling across the pavement. Evan landed his fist into Darien's side, grinning at the sick thud of impact as he felt bones give way to his knuckles. Darien coughed and winced as he straightened himself. He seemed to be in a lot of pain. He growled as he charged Evan again.

This time Darien hit Evan in the side of the face and followed through with the rest of his body. He tackled Evan to the ground and bore down on him. Evan held his arms up to protect from Darien's savage blows and wrestled to get free. The heat radiating off Darien was intense, and Evan feared he was preparing to shift.

If Darien shifted in this position, it would not matter whether anyone saw them or not because Evan would be dead by that point. There was no doubt Darien would rip him open at the belly before Evan could get free.

Evan used all of his strength to throw Darien off of him. He could see the wildness in Darien's eyes, that golden flash of the animal inside of him bursting to get out. It sparked the beast within Evan's own chest and he could feel the transformation coming on.

He clenched his fists and tried to subdue it, but the urge was far too strong. He could feel his muscles rippling under his clothes and the beginning of a roar rumble in his chest.

Darien's eyes went wide and he scrambled away from Evan on the sidewalk.

Evan felt his shirt rip as his body grew too big for it. Tufts of fur sprouted around his head and claws burst out from the ends of his newly-formed paws. He roared and snarled as he shook the tatters of cloth from his body.

Darien kept increasing the distance between them, his hands out as if trying to ward Evan away. But for Evan there was no turning back. He was barely aware of his own thoughts, only the urge to bite and tear spurring him on.

He pounced. Darien fled down the sidewalk, Evan's claws barely missing the flesh of his back. Evan's paws pounded against the pavement as he chased the man, his mane flying wild around his head. Darien suddenly turned and disappeared into a nearby building.

Evan skidded and hit a lamp post. When he finally righted himself, Darien was already out of sight. Evan could not follow him into the building, knowing his size advantage would become a liability in the closed quarters of the apartment building. He was built for battle on an open savanna, not the labyrinthine corridors of cheap LA housing.

Evan slunk away from the building, suddenly overwhelmed with disappointment. He had let Darien provoke him into shifting, and Evan now knew just how tenuous his control of his own emotions was. It had always been a problem when Evan was young, his quick temper and constant need to prove his dominance. And Lily had brought it all flooding back. *Why couldn't he control himself?*

Having torn through his clothes during the transformation, Evan would now have to navigate the late-night LA streets in his lion form. He kept to the alleyways, alert to every sound around him. Broken glass cut into his paws as he skirted a row of dumpsters, and the foul stench of rotting eggs filled his nose.

Despite his foul surroundings, his movements were graceful and dignified.

He was a flash of brilliant gold moving through the city, weaving his way ever steadily west towards his home in Beverly Grove.

By the time he got home, he was exhausted. He quietly transformed at the back of the building and used the fire access stairs to get to his apartment. He slid open his bedroom window and climbed into the room, feeling the ache of every muscle as he lowered himself onto the floor. The soles of his feet were tender from the shards of glass he had walked over earlier as he tiptoed to the bathroom.

Running the tap on hot, he stepped into the shower. Steam quickly filled the air as he stood motionless under the torrent of water. The water ran in rivulets down between the locks of hair on his forehead and into the cut made by Darien's ring, stinging the raw flesh while it washed it clean.

Evan barely noticed. He was only thinking of Lily. Did Al also know about Lily, and was that why he was so eager to corrupt Evan and his brother? Maybe Al was trying to get the competition out of the way so that Darien could take his mate without interference. Al had always been close to Darien, slinking around in Darien's shadow like a good little beta and helping him whenever he could.

Al seemed to think that his favors would be repaid once Darien rose to the position of alpha in the pride and did everything he could to ensure that it happened. But Evan knew that Darien did not need the help.

Darien was a snake, cunning and dangerously alluring, and notorious for using his charms against women. His good looks had lured many astray and Evan knew Lily would be just as susceptible if she wasn't careful. She was young, naïve, and still star-struck by her new Hollywood life. She had dreams of being famous and Darien would feed into them until he had her wrapped around his finger.

Evan had been too passive. Lately he had been waiting for Lily to come to him, when he should have been chasing her down. For now, it seemed Darien was only stalking her, biding his time until he had an opening to make her his. But it was only a matter of time before Darien closed in. Before that happened, Evan needed to offer Lily something Darien couldn't. But what that was, Evan had no idea.

Like a whisper, his father's words came back to him. He was not in love with Lily, nor had he any intention of becoming so. Attachment was not something Evan was good at, nor something he particularly wanted. He liked the intoxication of sexual attraction and the adventure of pursuing new women.

The only difference between Lily and the others was purely genetic. It was an animal need that drew him to her, nothing more. She had the genes his pride needed. He couldn't afford to get wrapped up in emotions now. It would only make him weak. He knew Darien could never love Lily, but he was not sure that he could either.

Evan shut off the water and stepped out of the shower, the heat from his skin spiraling up in visible wisps of steam. He pulled a towel around his waist and stood in front of the mirror. The reflection staring back at him looked tired, almost sad. His amber eyes held a tinge of uncertainty that he did not like to see in himself.

He leaned towards the mirror, looking over the cut on his forehead. It was pretty deep and would likely need stitches. Evan riffled through the cabinet under the kitchen sink and found a half-empty box of butterfly bandages. He used a couple to close the cut, wincing as the adhesive pulled his skin taut.

There was no way he would be able to act with such an ugly injury on his face, and the director would be furious with him for getting injured and messing up the shooting schedule. But that was the least of his worries.

In the bedroom, Evan replaced his towel with a pair of boxer shorts and collapsed onto his bed. Lying down above the covers, he stared at the ceiling until sleep stole over him. He dreamed no dreams that he could remember, but when he woke in the morning Lily's name was on his lips.

"What happened to you?" Lily asked. Evan was sporting a nasty cut on his brow. She had not seen him on set all morning and she suspected that this was the reason.

"It's nothing," Evan replied. "Just me being clumsy."

"I didn't know lions could be clumsy."

They were sitting outside a deli near the studio, Lily still wearing her wardrobe from shooting that morning and Evan in one of the well-fitted t-shirts he favored. Since Evan didn't have any scenes today, he had asked Lily to lunch in a surprising gesture that Lily had dared to hope was a sign of their growing closeness outside the bedroom. Because Lily had to work, she had insisted that they meet near the studio for lunch. Though she felt bad making Evan come out here on his day off, she didn't want to pass up the chance to spend time with him.

She watched him pull a loose piece of bacon from his sandwich and pop it in his mouth.
"Is that why the director changed the shooting schedule?" she asked.

"Yeah," Evan replied after he had finished chewing. "He yelled at me for about an hour on the phone yesterday. Apparently, I'm causing him a lot of stress." He smiled charmingly.

Lily took a sip of her lemonade. "Well, it's no fun on the set without you. I hope you can come back soon."

"Yeah, me too."

Lily couldn't help but notice how Evan's eyes never lingered long on her. He kept looking around the street as if he were expecting someone.

"Hey," she said as his eyes followed a passing car. "Thanks for walking me home the other night. I'm sorry you couldn't stay for breakfast. I'm actually a pretty good cook. Maybe you can come over again sometime. I'll cook for you."

"Uh-huh," Evan replied.

He seemed to be distracted by something behind her. Lily was starting to feel invisible. Why had he invited her to lunch if he was only going to ignore her? *Maybe,* Lily thought with amusement, *under all that masculine bravado he was really just shy*. He didn't know how to open up. Lily was determined to help him do so.

"Can we play a game?"

Evan furrowed his brows. "A game?"

"Yeah, I've been in character too long. It'll help me get back into my own skin for a while." Lily smiled an unassuming smile.

"What kind of game?" Evan asked.

"It's pretty simple. We take turns asking each other questions and answering them, but we're not allowed to ask a question that's been asked before. For example, if I ask your salary you can't ask mine. And you have to answer truthfully."

"Yeah, sure," Evan replied, though his eyes were still fixed on their surroundings rather than Lily. She didn't let it bother her.

"OK, I'll go first. Where were you born?"

"Los Angeles, and I've never left since," Evan replied without looking at her.

Lily was trying to get him comfortable before she started asking the real questions, but his lack of engagement was making her rethink her strategy. Her next question would have to require a more thoughtful answer.

"Your turn," she said.

"Why did you want to become an actress?" Evan asked, his eyes still fixed on some distant point.

The question threw Lily off, and she suddenly felt like the spotlight had been placed on her. She struggled for an answer, and her prolonged silence prompted Evan to look at her.

"There must be a reason, right? You didn't move all the way out here on a whim."

Lily toyed with the corner of the napkin in her lap. She regretted not being able to ask Evan the same question. Self-consciously she explained, "I've always loved acting, ever since I was a kid. I know it sounds kind of lame, but it's more than that. Where I grew up, there was nothing. I was stuck in the same place with the same people, and there wasn't much opportunity for excitement.

"But when I was acting, I could travel anywhere and have all sorts of life experiences right there on stage. And best of all, there were no consequences. I could fall in love with abandon and feel the heartbreak of loss, the rage of jealousy, and express all those emotions to their fullest without the fear of repercussions.

Because once the curtain went down, or the movie finished, I was no longer that character. I didn't have to live with the long-term burden of anything my characters experienced."

She fell silent with a shy smile. Evan had turned his attention entirely upon her as she spoke and was now regarding her with a look of intense interest.

Lily's brain was whirring. Had she said something strange? Had she spoken too much? With no reaction to go off of, Lily was feeling even more unsure of herself.

"Your turn," was all he said.

"Okay, what did you want to be when you were a kid?"

"A baseball player," Evan answered without hesitation. "My dad's a huge Dodgers fan and I always dreamed of making the major leagues when I was in school, but then he told me he'd stop watching baseball if I ever went professional. He said it's an unfair advantage for guys like us, shifters, to use our strength and abilities to get ahead in sports.

"No matter how hard the others trained, they would never achieve the level I naturally possessed. It just wasn't sportsmanlike. So, I stopped playing baseball and went into acting instead."

Something about his mention of the Dodgers gave Lily vague recollections of hearing the name elsewhere recently, but she could not fix on anything solid before Evan asked his next question.

"What kind of person do you imagine yourself marrying?"

Lily nearly spilled her glass of water as she took a sip. The question had come out of the blue. What could possibly be his motive for asking such a thing? Maybe he was playing with her, to see if she would describe someone similar to Evan. That way he could gauge how attached she was to him and decide if it was time to bail. He didn't seem like the monogamous type, let alone a husband.

She said, "I'd like to marry someone responsible, a man who's got my back but won't push me in any particular direction. But he has to be strong, too, someone I can depend on no matter what. And he has to be romantic, and spontaneous, and not too set in his ways."

Lily wondered if she sounded too picky. But marriage was a big deal. A woman had to be picky. Luckily for Evan, he was only a fling. Lily could afford to compromise on a few of his less charming points.

"Is that everything?" Evan asked. His brow was still furrowed. He was taking this game far more seriously than Lily had expected, or maybe she had said too much after all.

Lily smiled, trying to lighten the mood. "I still haven't decided whether being a shifter's a deal-breaker or not," she joked.

Evan's frown lessened but it did not give way to a full smile. "Okay, let me know when you decide. It's your turn," he said.

Lily glanced at the time on her phone as she thought of her question. Her lunch break was almost over. There was so much she wanted to ask him, and she was curious to hear Evan's next question as well. It seemed the more she found out about him the more puzzling he became.

But what she really wanted to know about was his shifting ability, and the others of his kind. It seemed that was the only personal aspect of Evan's life that he was willing to share with her openly.

Lily's question was cut off by a syrupy sweet voice calling Evan's name from somewhere behind her. Evan looked startled and half-stood from his chair. Lily turned to see a woman she vaguely recognized sauntering up to them from between tables. Her long hair swished behind her as she walked. She gave Lily a wink.

"Hey handsome," the woman said to Evan.

Evan sat back down in his chair uneasily, looking like he had been caught doing something bad.

"Jade, what are you doing here?"

Jade ignored his question and smiled at Lily. It was a razor-sharp smile that put Lily on edge. "Nice to see you again. I wondered how long he'd keep you around."

"Jade, don't be like that," Evan said. "We're just having lunch."

Jade continued to ignore him. "New costar, right? How long have you two been hooking up?"

"You don't need to answer that," Evan said, looking at Lily. His scowl told her this woman was more than just his agent, if that hadn't been a lie as well.

Jade put a finger to her lower lip and frowned. "It's just girls talk, Evan. I didn't think you were such a prude. After all, it's not like your affairs are any secret. I just wanted to know if you've been fucking her since before or after your first onscreen kiss."

Lily shrunk in her chair, wanting to become invisible.

"I mean," the woman continued. "It would be a waste of my time if things are serious between you two. I wouldn't want to become the third wheel."

There was anger in Evan's tone. "You're not involved in this. There's nothing between us, and there hasn't been for years. I'm sure you have plenty of other exes you could be harassing right now."

The woman seemed to be one of Evan's ex-girlfriends. But then why had she been in Evan's trailer the other day? If they still had things to work through, Lily did not want to be a part of it. She tried to excuse herself as the two continued to argue. "Evan, I've got to get back on set. I'll see you around, okay?"

She stood from her chair and, setting a ten-dollar bill down on the table to pay for her share of lunch, hurried away from the bickering pair before Evan could protest. The sounds of their angry voices followed her down the street.

* * *

The basement was thick with cigarette smoke, its acrid stench clawing at Evan's lungs. There were no windows to let the smoke out so it hung in clouds over the men hunched over stacks of papers, the numbers scrawled on them corresponding to bets made for games of chance already rigged one way or another.

Al lurked somewhere in the back, his thin shadow barely visible through all the smoke. Evan waited for Al to come to him, the mad thump of blood in his temple playing the bass beat over the incessant clacking of calculator keys around him. The men paid Evan no notice.

Whether it was horse racing or local boxing matches, Al's pride knew who would win at least a week before all the bets were in. These men in the basement were part of the accounting branch, responsible for taking bets from hapless suckers who didn't know the games were decided beforehand.

Al's pride had its tendrils dug into enough boxing coaches and racetrack supervisors that any number of mishaps could lead to the favored champion suddenly being disqualified or losing a match. Over the years, they had raked in hundreds of thousands on such scams, and yet they still lived in the armpit of the city,

perhaps because this was where they thrived best. The money was not the goal for them, the power was. They felt they ran the city from the underground.

Al cut a path through the cigarette smog, his wiry but strong arms waving about to clear the air in front of him. His long hair was slicked straight back and greasy from whatever kept it there. Evan felt dirty just looking at him.

"I could get the cops to shut you down," Evan said lightly as if commenting on the weather. He had to bluff that he had the upper hand when really it was Al holding the royal flush.

Al smirked. "Is that why you've come here? To get me thrown in jail? You're not the first one to try, but if you do you'll find out just how much of the LAPD we own."

Evan ignored the obvious bait. "I'm here to talk about Darien."

"Then you should talk to him directly. I don't make decisions for our alpha."

"He's not your alpha. Last I checked, his father was."

"The old man's in the hospital, didn't you hear? His heart's not working so well these days. Darien's acting alpha. He makes the decisions for us."

Evan swore. Darien's father and the patriarch of the pride's strongest family, was a man from the old world who still remembered a life outside the crime-riddled streets of LA and who possessed a wisdom only age could achieve. To hear that he was having medical problems was yet another strike against Evan. He had been hoping to talk to the old man at some point.

"Give me the name of the hospital. I want to see him."

"And what if I don't want you to?"

Al crossed his arms over his chest in an insolent, almost childish gesture and Evan wanted to punch him. Evan instead swallowed his anger, reminding himself of his dangerous outburst the night before.

"I already warned Darien about this, but war's coming if he doesn't back down."

"What are you talking about?"

"Don't play dumb with me," Evan growled. "You doubled rent on my brother and got him to use again just to get me out of the way. The timing's too perfect. You know Darien and I are both after Lily. And you're trying to rig the competition against me, just like you always do." Evan swept his hands to either side of him while the men at the tables kept calculating away.

Al made a perfunctory glance at the workers. "If you've got us all figured out, then why don't you make a stand for your mate? Challenge Darien to a fight like the animals we are. It's the easiest way to resolve this."

Evan knew such a fight would be vicious, even deadly. Things had been close enough outside of Lily's apartment the other night with Darien poised to kill him. Darien's strength was equal to his own and Evan could not be sure he would win a fair fight. He couldn't bear thinking of what would happen to Lily if Darien won.

He crossed his own arms, mirroring Al's posture. But it was not the closed, defensive gesture that Al had made. It was rather one of power. He said, "I don't want the feud between our prides to end in the bloodshed of our kind. We've already drawn enough of each other's blood." His eyes fixed on Al's scar to punctuate his point. "I'm willing to cut you a deal if you can get Darien under control."

Al looked nervous, but interested nonetheless. "What kind of deal?" he asked tentatively.

"How would you like to become the next alpha?"

Al was clearly caught off-guard. He fumbled in his pockets for a pack of cigarettes and nearly crushed it in a shaking fist. Evan waited for him to take out a cigarette and light it before continuing. He had hit a weak spot.

"You and I both know you're the one who keeps the pride going. Darien may be the one who gets all the credit, but you put in the hours. When was the last time he went out into the streets himself to make a deal? He profits off drugs and stolen goods but keeps his hands clean.

"Your current alpha, his father, is much more like you. He built the empire you're set to inherit through his own grit and hard work. He always took responsibility for his pride. I remember those years when he was in jail, when we were just kids and Darien had to go to your house after school because there was no one home to take care of him.

"If Darien becomes your pride's leader, who do you think he's going to throw under the bus if the LAPD suddenly decides to put a stop to your illegal operations? He's not going to take responsibility like his father did. You'll be the one rotting in the state prison while Darien enjoys life outside."

Al's panicked inhales had left his cigarette a smoldering stub. He flicked it onto the basement's cement floor and lit another one. This time, his breaths were slow and even. He measured his words as he said them. "You know, I can't decide who I hate more, you or Darien," he said with a look of distaste.

"You must be stupid if you think I'd fall for something like that. I'd never beat Darien in a fight for dominance. You're too scared to challenge him and you've got fifty pounds on me. There's nothing you can do to make me alpha and we both know it."

"That's it, then? You're not even going to try?"

Al scoffed. "Like I said, there's no chance in hell."

"Okay, but at least stop encouraging Jade. It's not healthy for her to keep obsessing over me like that. She's going to get herself into trouble."

"Jade?" Al asked innocently. "Oh yeah, she came around here the other day asking about you. I hadn't seen her in forever. I think she's under Darien's employ these days. But if you're trying to blame her on me, don't waste your breath. She's all your doing. If you'd never strung her along in the first place she wouldn't be your problem. Now if you're done wasting my time, I've got business to attend to."

Al disappeared back through the smoke, leaving Evan feeling like he wanted to rip a hole through the man's chest. He stomped up the stairs from the basement to the bar, the one he had gotten in a fight with Al inside only weeks ago. Now, it was an empty husk, the doors not set to open for another couple of hours. The only light came from a dim row of red bulbs above the bar and the neon beer signs in the front windows.

On the way out, Evan crashed into someone. He turned to tell the guy to watch where he was going, but his words fell away when he realized who it was. His brother stood in the doorway looking like he had just been hit across the face. There were papers clutched in his hand.

He spoke before Evan had a chance to get angry all over again. "I'm leaving the apartment. I'm bringing the lease termination letter for Al to sign. We're moving back in with Dad." He took an instinctive step back from his brother but he kept the bar door open as if to invite Evan's response.

Evan could see the papers in his hand were indeed part of a rent contract, but he doubted the words printed on the page meant anything to Al and his cronies. "You really think that's going to get you out? Contracts mean nothing to them. They don't play by the rules." he shouted. He was still in a rage from his conversation with Al and was more than ready to take it all out on his brother.

"Dad said he'll come down here if he has to. If they won't listen to me, they'll listen to him."

Evan pulled his brother back out the door. He didn't want to be overheard by any of the snakes inside the bar. He hissed into his brother's ear, "They're after our pride because there's a woman they want. A woman who I intend to claim for myself."

Matt pushed Evan away from him. "Then why don't you let them have her?"

"Because she's mine."

"What does that even mean?"

Evan was thrown by his brother's question. His words had seemed clear enough. "I found her first, I'm the closest to her, and I intend to make her my mate."

Matt ran a hand through his wavy dark hair, one of the few traits he shared with his younger brother. "Can I talk to you, man to man?"

Evan shrugged.

"I'm married. I have a kid. I know Dad probably gave you some speech about how he won Mom for the pride, and how love doesn't matter when choosing your mate, but it's all bullshit. Mom loved

Dad because he stood up for her. When those vultures came to take her away he was there to protect her.

"Even if he had lost the fight, she still would have been his mate because it's not entirely up to the men to decide. Sure, he and Mom would have been kicked out of the pride and forced to leave Los Angeles, but it would have been worth it. Strength and status aren't everything in this world.

"If your plan was to knock this girl up and then dump her when her usefulness to the pride has run its course, that makes you no different from Darien. We might be animals, but animals can love, too. If there's any part of you that feels even a little bit of affection for this woman, you won't let her be used like this. You'll fight for her, but not like beasts. You'll fight for her heart."

When his speech was finished, Matt had regained in his posture and his expression showed much of the dignity he used to possess as a young lion. Evan recalled the older brother he used to look up to, before all of the trouble with the drugs and Al's pride. Evan didn't know what to say. He pictured his brother as a screw-up, someone whose life was just a series of bumbling failures.

He never imagined his brother giving him advice, especially not with such insight as this.

He felt even more terrible for taking the role of alpha out from under his brother. Maybe if he had waited a few years, Matt would have straightened out to where he would have been able to take over for their father as head of the pride. But now that Evan held that role, the only way Matt could take it was through a physical fight. And that wouldn't happen.

Evan let his brother disappear into the bar without a word. He stood on the sidewalk feeling more lost than he ever had in his life. He had been stupid, treating Lily like she was a fresh kill on the savanna, something to devour before the other lions came circling in. But she was a woman—a beautiful, talented, strong woman who somehow put up with his asshole behavior though she had no good reason to.

Were things more simple, he would let her go, realizing that he was not nearly good enough for her and was only holding her back. But he couldn't afford to do that. If he stopped seeing her, Darien would take it as a sign of surrender, that Evan had abandoned Lily for Darien to take. And Darien would not treat her kindly. As long as Evan was seen as a threat, Darien would at least keep his hands off her until the matter was settled one way or another. And Evan had every intention of winning.

CHAPTER SEVEN

Lily's phone rang. She had been running lines with Tessa in their apartment most of the afternoon, and the two of them were now in the kitchen baking bread as their patience for focusing on the script had run out. She didn't recognize the number calling and debated letting it ring, but worried it might be something to do with work.

The cut on Evan's eyebrow was starting to heal, and with some luck in a few days it would be healed enough for makeup to be able to hide it well enough to resume filming. She wondered if someone was calling about the revised shooting schedule. She wiped her flour-dusted hands on a towel and picked up.

"Hello?" she said.

"Hey, it's me."

"Who is it?" Tessa asked loudly.

"Evan," Lily replied, cupping her hand over the receiver. She recognized him by voice, though it wasn't his phone number. She asked him about it.

"Oh, yeah sorry. I lost my phone the other day, when we met for lunch. This is just a replacement until I can get it back."

Lily didn't like being reminded of that day at the café. She had wanted to know about Evan's past, but not necessarily his old flames. Those kinds of memories were better left untouched.

"I almost didn't pick up. Have you checked with the café? Maybe you left it there."

"I called them but they hadn't seen it. I must have dropped it on the street. That, or someone nicked it while I wasn't looking."

Tessa had abandoned her work in the kitchen and was watching Lily as she talked on the phone. "Why's he calling from a weird number?"

Lily waved her away.

"We never finished that game," Evan said. "How about I pick you up in a half hour and we can continue where we left off?"

The evening sun was just barely starting to sink down in the sky, and Lily realized she was hungry. Dinner with Evan sounded great. "Sure," she replied. "But can you make it an hour? I haven't been out of the apartment all day and I'm a mess."

"Are you going on a date?" Tessa asked in an obnoxiously loud voice.

Evan had apparently heard her, and was laughing.

"Yeah, it's a date," he replied.

Lily's heart raced. He had never used the word date before, a term their relationship did not seem to fit. She let herself hope that things were about to change.

"But it really does have to be a half hour," Evan said. "Or else we'll miss it."

"Miss what?" Lily asked.

"You'll see," Evan said and hung up.

Lily was left with feelings of curiosity and apprehension. But she had no time to dwell on these feelings as she had a date to get ready for.

As promised, Evan was at her door half an hour from the moment he had hung up. In that time, Lily had managed to change into a fresh blouse and skirt, and Tessa helped her run a brush through her hair and braid it into a loose updo.

Not knowing the dress code for where they were going, Lily opted for nice but casual. She hoped it would be enough.

Evan himself was wearing plain jeans and a t-shirt, though the jeans were cut well and the t-shirt was a crisp white. Lily envied how effortlessly men like him could put together an outfit.

"Ready to go?" he asked with an inviting smile.

Evan's car was parked at the curb outside. The only other time Lily had seen it was the night they had first hooked up. It seemed like ages ago, before she knew about his secret and before she had really started falling for him.

She loved the car's black silhouette, its silver trim and long, sleek design. She had never been especially interested in cars before, but the deep, purring sound of the engine as the car idled at a stop light made her feel like she had fallen into a different time.

She watched Evan as he drove, his strong hands gripping the wheel and his amber eyes watching the road ahead. An errant lock of hair bounced against his forehead as he turned to look at her.

"I'm sorry about the other day," Evan said, his voice sounding oddly loud after the long silence. "I didn't think she would show up."

"Your ex?" Lily asked.

Evan nodded. "I think Jade's jealous of you because she knows you're different from the others."

"How so?"

"I care about you." The words set Lily's heartbeat racing. "Ever since I first kissed you, you've been the only woman on my mind. As soon as I saw you there on set the first time, I knew you were special and I just had to have you."

Lily smiled, though she couldn't help but doubt the full truth of his words. "So, I'm not just another one of your on-set affairs? You seem to have quite a reputation around the studio, you know."

Evan adjusted his hands on the wheel. "Maybe I want to try something new." Lily smiled.
He looked uncomfortable and changed the subject. "Remember when I took you to see the sunrise, and told you the Hollywood sign was better at sunset?"

They were driving along Mulholland drive towards Hollywood, following the ridge of mountains as the road curved above the city. Cars zipped past on the opposite lane and with each came a rush of wind through the open windows that ruffled Lily's hair.

"Of course I remember," she said. "Is that where we're going?"

Evan nodded and pulled into a small scenic overlook that had a view of the Los Angeles basin and beyond it the famous sign with its white letters reflecting the orange sunlight.

Evan got out of the car. "This is why I couldn't wait an hour. We would have missed the sunset."

Lily joined him on the hood of the car, her butt against the warm metal. Evan put his arm around her as they watched the ant-like cars fly down the 101 into the valley. Far in the distance, the skyline of downtown was just visible. The skyscrapers stood dark against the orange sky. Looking down on the city like this made it feel all at once both small and immense, but Lily felt like she was finally finding her place in it.

She nestled into the crook of Evan's arm as the golden sun sank lower and lower in the sky, taking on a deep pink hue as it dipped towards the horizon. The letters of the Hollywood sign blushed crimson before eventually fading and going dark. The loss of the sun allowed the lights in the valley to shine brightly, the city coming alive after a long sleep in the summer sun.

Evan stretched and leaned back against the car, propping himself up with his elbows.

Lily turned to him. "You said we had a game to finish."

Evan scratched the back of his head looking rather bashful. "I guess I should keep my promise. Who's turn was it, anyway?"

"I believe it was mine." On the way over, Lily had been thinking up questions to ask him. She thought that maybe his invitation to her tonight was an indication that he was ready to open up to her. She asked, "What was it like growing up here? I mean, having the power you have, it couldn't have been easy."

Evan sat up and leaned forward. He studied his hands before meeting her gaze again. "The city's so big, there's a lot that goes on unseen. You'd be surprised at how easily even lions can be ignored, especially when you've got as many connections in the city as my family does."

"So your family's important?"

"That's two questions," Evan protested.

"But you haven't answered my first yet."

Evan sighed. "If I tell you about this stuff, about my family and how I grew up, it might change how you think about me. I'm not that person anymore and I don't want to lose you because of it."

The vulnerability in Evan's expression was something Lily had never seen in him before. She leaned in until their lips were touching, reassuring him with her kiss. When they broke apart there was a new fire in Evan's eyes.

He said, "You probably have this glamorous image of me, but when I was a kid I had nothing. I grew up on the streets of downtown LA spending most of my time fighting and getting into trouble. My family never had much money, but we've lived in the city long enough that we know how to cover our tracks. Being a lion in a city full of men can get a shifter into trouble real fast.

"But my family aren't the only shifters in LA. There's another pride, and they're much more dangerous than us. My older brother and I grew up with a couple of their boys. Darien and Al got into some pretty bad stuff and I probably would have to if I hadn't decided to make something of myself and become an actor."

Lily gasped at the mention of Darien's name. It could be just a coincidence, but she had to be sure. "Did you say Darien?" she asked.

"Yeah, why?" Evan replied slowly. The look of concern on his face made Lily all the more uneasy. "Do you know him?"

"He's a tall guy with a beard, right? He was stalking me a while back." Lily didn't know how to put it more delicately. And if this man had something to do with Evan, it was better if he knew everything.

Evan stood from the car's hood looking visibly irritated. "Did he hurt you?" he asked.
"He tried to," Lily said. "The first time we met. He cornered me in an alley but I got away. Then he followed me in Hollywood when I was there with Tessa and tried to apologize, but I told him to stay away from me and I haven't seen him since."

Evan grabbed Lily's hands and looked intently into her eyes. "Darien is a dangerous man," he warned. "If you see him again, you need to call me immediately. The cops aren't going to help you. His pride has underground connections everywhere. Everything that comes out of that man's mouth is a lie, and he only wants to hurt you."

Lily was startled by the sudden warning. She didn't know how to reply. All she could do was nod and promise to be careful, and hope she never had the misfortune of meeting Darien again.

The two of them fell silent as they got back into the car. Evan seemed preoccupied with his own thoughts, but as he drove he started to talk to Lily about his past and his brother, and how Darien and a man named Al had caused all sorts of trouble for them. It seemed that even among shifters there was a lot of bad blood, and some were more dangerous than others.

It seemed an impossible burden that Evan carried on his shoulders, being the alpha of his pride while also trying to pursue his acting career and escape his troubled past. Lily wondered how he could have done it alone all this time, and was glad she could now share some of the pain. He had finally let her in, allowing love to bloom where there had only been sexual attraction before. Lily did not know what had brought on the sudden change, and she could only look forward to what was to come.

* * *

Evan was in the shower again, his favorite place to mull things over. Though this time his thoughts were mostly positive, for the first time in what seemed like forever. He had finally opened himself up to Lily and it had felt like a huge relief. She knew about all of him, not just the glossy magazine cover version or the predatory animal hiding inside. She knew about where he came from, about all the pain hidden in his past and his struggle to heal since.

He had also managed to warn her about Darien, and now that she was on her guard, he would not be able to get to her. The only thing he had kept from her was his original motivation for pursuing her. Now that he had fallen for her, his animal desire for her felt almost obscene. Matt had been right. Up until now he had been just as bad as Darien, pursuing Lily for his own selfish purposes. He had never known love before, and it took experiencing it firsthand to realize just how important it really was.

A faint sound came over the rush of water, the high ringing buzz of the front doorbell. Evan was not expecting visitors and could not think of who it might be. It wasn't Lily, that was for sure. And his family didn't know where he lived. Well, they knew the neighborhood but they never had any reason to visit him. It was always him checking up on them.

He let the water run for a while longer, waiting for the buzzer to ring again as the water cascaded past his ears and muffled out most of the sound. There was a pause, then more buzzing and then the buzzes turned to brisk knocking. Evan wondered who it could possibly be that was so insistent on seeing him. He turned off the water and dried himself off with a towel. Water was still dripping from his hair as he left the bathroom with the towel wrapped around his waist.

He almost had a heart attack seeing the woman standing in his living room. She had her back to him, busying herself with a bottle of whiskey and two tumblers full of ice.

"Jade, what the hell are you doing in my house?"

Jade turned, her long hair moving like oil with her body's momentum. She smiled and put a hand on her hip, holding the other out with a glass of whiskey towards Evan. "I'm here to apologize," she said.

"Well I don't want you here. I'm calling the cops."

"Just take the drink," Jade pouted. "I heard you went to see Al and I want to make you a counter offer. You and I both know I don't have a reputation for loyalty. Let me give you a chance to use that to your advantage. I've decided I like Lily. I'm on your side here, and I want to help."

Evan glared at Jade but took the drink anyway. The smell of the alcohol was stronger than usual somehow, as if she had spilled some while pouring the drinks. He stepped away from her again quickly, not trusting her even at arm's length. He answered, "If you were on my side, you wouldn't have broken into my apartment."

"I didn't break in here. Your spare key was inside your car. Okay, maybe I broke into your car to get to it but you wouldn't have let me in otherwise."

Evan remembered vividly why Jade no longer had a pride. She was chaotic, uninhibited, and seemed to think that consequences could not reach her.

"I can still call the cops," Evan warned, though his tone had lost most of its edge. As he sipped his drink he started to feel the worry slipping away. He would not make an enemy out of Jade today if he could help it. That fight at the café had given him enough of a headache. If he was civil, maybe she would leave all the more quickly.

"You said you wanted to help me. Why?"

Jade licked the rim of her glass where a stray drop of whiskey had sat. "I don't know, I got bored. I'm tired of working for Al and I want out. You're a big-time movie star, so I though you could help me."

Evan was feeling a little dizzy, perhaps from confusion at Jade's sudden turn of heart or the blood rushing to his head from the hot shower and alcohol, and sat down on the sofa. His damp towel was uncomfortable underneath his legs and he was starting to wish he had put on some clothes.

"So, you're going to help me?" he asked.

He gripped the arm rest of the sofa. He felt like he was sweating too much. He barely heard Jade's answer through the pump of blood in his ears.

Jade only smiled at him, her eyes watching him closely. Evan felt a sense of dread like something was very wrong. His jaw kept clenching and he couldn't stop sweating though the room was cool and he was wearing only a towel.

She was on him before Evan could move away. One leg straddled the sofa's arm rest while the other lay between his legs. She leaned down close, her lips almost brushing his ear. He shivered, but not in excitement. There was something odd about her smell. Evan felt suddenly hot, almost sick. It was then he recognized it.

"Do you like my perfume?" Jade hissed. "Al brewed it up for me. Lily's pheromones at ten times the strength. But you have to be close to smell it. I think it goes well with the ecstasy I put in your drink."

Evan's brain was swimming. His brain failed to process the words even as his body was feeling the full effects of the drugs. He threw his still half-full tumbler to the floor.

Jade laughed.

"That's not going to help. You already drank plenty before you even started talking to me. I stopped by this morning on my way to work. The pills needed time to dissolve."

Evan recalled in horror the drinks he'd had before hopping in the shower. There was no way he could have known they were spiked. The drugs had been in his system for almost an hour now and he was nearing the edge of the drop into the rabbit hole. There was no turning back now.

He hated Jade for tricking him, for not letting him go even after all these years. He tried to fixate on this anger and use it to fight the effects of the drugs. But the anger itself started to dissolve away, leaving only a sense of understanding.

He felt himself opening up to the world around him, the weight of worry and judgment fleeing from his consciousness. Maybe this was an opportunity to connect with Jade on a deeper level and give her a chance to finally let go. He was aware he was smiling.

Jade's laughter was like music, a dangerous siren's song. "It looks like it's doing its job. I guess I should go get ready." She walked to the front door and unlocked it.

Evan couldn't figure out why, but it didn't seem to matter to him. Nothing really mattered, except the look on Jade's face as she turned back towards him.

He moved towards her feeling like an arrow drawn to a target, but stopped partway remembering Lily and the promise he had made to her. He fought against the arousal, telling himself it was the artificial product of the chemicals surging through his body. The image of Lily's face swam up from the drugged depths of his consciousness. He closed his eyes and breathed in her scent, strengthening the association between her pheromones and his feelings for her. It was starting to work. His resolve was returning.

He could feel Jade's fingers gently stroking his chest. The feeling of her skin against his sent electric chills through his body. He backed up instinctively, though he yearned for more. She touched him again and the chills turned to waves of pleasure.

His sense of touch had never been so alive. Jade pushed him backwards onto the soft carpeting of the living room, straddling his middle with her thighs. The animal inside him was awake and clawing to get out. Evan tugged at the towel around his waist, feeling the soft fabric glide against his fingers like the fur of a kitten.

"Not so fast," Jade said as she put her hands over his, stopping them from removing the towel. "We can't start the show until we know the audience is on its way."

She reached into the back pocket of her jeans and took out a phone. Evan recognized it as his and tried to take it from her. She pulled it out of the way and Evan stopped trying.

The ecstasy told him it didn't really matter who had his phone, anyway. At least he knew where it was. Jade typed out a message and within seconds the phone dinged with a reply. She smiled satisfactorily and threw the phone off to the side.

"Okay, where were we?" she said, looking down at Evan with a suggestive smile.

She pulled off her shirt, revealing a lacy black bra underneath. Evan wondered how the fabric would feel under his fingers, now that his sense of touch was dialed up to ten. Jade moved his hands up her stomach towards her bra. She leaned down and her long hair fell like a curtain over the both of them. Evan was aware of nothing but the sensation of her skin and the intimate darkness around them.

A knock on Evan's front door took him out of the moment. Jade sat up and turned towards the door. Evan used the distraction to try to fix on Lily's image in his mind. He fought the invading thoughts that the drugs were bringing to him with the determination only someone in love could possess.

"I told her she could come right in," Jade said as she turned back to Evan and started to unhook her bra.

He squeezed his eyes shut, feeling suddenly ill and wanting to escape. But the dazed lethargy of his body made his bones feel like lead and his muscles unusable goop.

The knocking stopped and the door opened with an almost inaudible click. Evan felt like he could feel the door handle turning inside his own body. Something in the back of his head warned him of danger, but his body still wouldn't move no matter how hard he willed it to.

"Evan?" Lily called into the room. There was a moment of silence, and then, "What are you doing here?" Her voice quivered with accusation.

Jade only laughed. The harsh, taunting sound of it flipped a switch in Evan's brain. He pushed the evil woman off of him and struggled to sit up.

He could see the look of betrayal in Lily's watery eyes. "Lily," he started.

"You told me you weren't seeing anyone else," she said, her tone cutting through the remaining fog in his brain.

His body, however, was still lagging behind. He stumbled to his feet and lost his balance, half-falling onto the sofa.

"No, it's not what it looks like." The age-old words of guilt tumbled out of his mouth before he could stop them. It really wasn't his fault. He was tricked.

Lily stood at the entryway of the living room, her arms crossed tight over her chest and her mouth fixed into a tight frown. Her bottom lip was quivering, trying to hold back the tears that threatened to burst forth.

Evan tried again. "Please, you have to understand. There are people out to get me. Jade came here to push us apart. She drugged me. She, she—"

Evan's words faded into silence. Everything sounded like a lie. Nothing he could do would change that. He was half-naked on the floor with another woman who Lily knew to have been involved with him. No words could overcome the damning evidence against him.

Lily turned away to leave.

"Wait!" Evan shouted. Lily ignored him and disappeared out the door.

Rage filled Evan, a deep anger towards the woman who had driven an irreparable wedge between himself and Lily. He shot a piercing glare at Jade who had been sitting on the sofa the whole time with a smug look on her face.

"You need to leave," he growled, throwing her discarded shirt at her with force.

Jade's smile receded from her face and she looked back at him with a glare of her own. "You can't have her, you know. Darien's made his claim on her and he's the strongest alpha in the city. He always gets what he wants. And anyway, the bitch isn't even a shifter. I'd make a much better mate for you."

Evan replied, "If I see you again, I'm calling a meeting of all the prides in LA and I'm going to get you kicked out of the city. Don't think that this fight with Darien can't be put aside for a second to deal with trash like you crawling the streets. Now that you've run out your usefulness with this little scheme of his, I'm sure he'll be happy to see the back of you, too."

Jade stood from the sofa with a huff and pulled her shirt down over her head, smoothing out the wrinkles as she walked away from Evan. The dark hair down her back was like a wall between them.

"All I did was love you," she said without turning around. "But you hate your past, and I'm a part of it. I realize that now and I won't bother you again."

As the front door clicked behind her, Evan punched one of the sofa cushions in frustration. Everything about that woman was a lie, from her supposed love for Evan to her dealings with Darien. He didn't entertain for a second that she had done this because she wanted him for herself.

He wondered what Darien had promised her. Would he stoop so low as to give her a place in his pride, just to get Evan out of the way? Now Lily was out there somewhere, hurt and angry at Evan. If he didn't try to explain things now, there would be no second chance. Evan ran to his bedroom and pulled on whatever clothes were laying around then headed straight for the door.

He had to find Lily before she went back to her apartment. There was no telling what would be waiting for her when she got there, and in such a vulnerable state she would be a prime target for whatever Darien had planned next.

Outside, a warm, dry breeze swept through the nighttime city, rustling trash cans and making the street lights sway slightly on their posts. It tugged at something inside of Evan, and though he knew he could cover more ground in his lion form, he forced himself to remain as he was. It couldn't have been more than fifteen minutes since Lily had left the apartment. But if she had driven here, she was probably already long gone.

Evan ran down the street on the off-chance she had parked somewhere far, but did not have to search long. Lily was sitting on the curb with her head in her hands, a nearby traffic signal flashing alternating reds and greens across her skin as the light changed. Evan approached cautiously and crouched down next to her. He gently put his arm across her shoulder.

She flinched and backed away, her hands moving from her face to reveal the streaks of tears down her red cheeks.

"How could you?" she asked. The blue of her irises were bright even in the darkness, their questioning gaze as deep as the ocean Evan felt himself drowning in.

Evan sunk down onto the curb, resting his elbows on his knees. He looked up at the traffic signal, which had again turned to red, to avoid having to meet Lily's gaze.

"I just, I want you to listen to what I have to say before you decide to judge me. There's a lot I've kept from you, but only because I was trying to protect you. The other pride, they want to hurt me. And they want to take you from me. What happened tonight was part of that, and it has nothing to do how I feel about you.

"I was tricked, drugged, but I swear I didn't touch her. I love you, Lily."

Though he had not meant to say it, he was telling the truth. Sitting next to him was the woman who had destroyed the walls around his past, who had seen into the most private parts of his life and had not judged him for them.

Of course he loved her.

Evan looked at Lily, waiting for a response, feeling open and raw and miserable from the drugs leaving his system. Everything had regained its normal cast, and the world was once more a dark place full of deception and lies. Evan just wanted to clear it all out and start over. Lily suddenly stood and started away from him down the sidewalk. Car keys jingled in her hand.

Evan stood up to follow her. "If you don't talk to me, I can't fix it," he called after her. "I just told you I love you, and I meant it. Can you at least look at me?"

Lily turned on her heels just as she reached her car. Her blue eyes locked on his. The anger in them hurt Evan in an almost physical way.

"What is there to fix?" she asked. "I'm not your girlfriend. Your actions have made that clear enough. Am I supposed to believe that you love me all of a sudden? You're lying through your teeth because you were caught red-handed. I saw her coming out of your trailer the other day. Don't think I'm that stupid."

"Please," Evan pleaded, "can we just go somewhere to talk? I'll explain everything."

"There's nothing more to say."

Lily wiped the fresh tears from her eyes and fumbled with her keys. She dropped them on the sidewalk and bent down to pick them up. Evan was there first and handed them back to her. She took them without thanks and got into her car.

Evan watched as she drove away, hating himself and Jade and pretty much everyone he knew except for Lily. It was his inescapable past that was now destroying the present. He had been stupid to think he could ever be anything more than the animal he was, that he could somehow break the pattern set by all of the generations before him.

But even if Lily hated him, he still had the responsibility of protecting her from Darien and any others who might want to take her. Now that there was no chance of Lily choosing him to be her mate, he would have to win her the old-fashioned way. He would have to challenge Darien to a fight.

CHAPTER EIGHT

He was a piece of scum, and she had been foolish to ever have fallen for him. She could have blamed it on his movie star charm, or the allure of his shape shifting ability, but deep down she knew it was because she was a small-town girl way out of her depth in the big city.

People were fake here, from their surgery-sculpted faces to their emotions, always trying to hide what was really inside. And though Evan had shown Lily a part of his true self, he had still conned her into thinking that she mattered to him.

She smacked the lump of dough on the counter with her fist. She had already baked four loaves of bread and was onto her fifth, the stack piling up on top of the oven as she took out her frustrations on the gooey mix of flour and water. Her hair flew wildly as she attacked the dough, her knuckles sinking into the surface with a satisfying thud. Tessa stood in the doorway to the bathroom with a curling iron wrapped in her hair.

"Maybe you should take a break," she said, unwrapping the curling iron and curling another section of hair around it. "There's no way we'll be able to eat all that bread. By we, I mean you, because I'm on a diet."

Lily gave the dough another good smack then stepped back from the counter. She wiped the hair away from her face with a flour-covered palm.

The curling iron clicked as Tessa continued to fix her hair. "You know, there are better ways to work off all that aggression."

"Like what?" Lily asked, her tone harsher than she had intended.

"Like, we could go out tonight. I'm thinking a loud club with cheap drinks, maybe that place down the street that's always blasting music all night."

"No thanks," Lily replied. She felt nothing like being in a room full of sweaty bodies and mindless dance music.

"I know, you're still upset about Evan. He's a bastard, but the best thing to do is move on as soon as you can. You can be sure that's what he's doing."

Lily felt tears welling in her eyes, remembering how she had found him with that woman in his apartment. True, they had still been mostly clothed at the time she had walked in, but had she arrived any later she had no doubt as to what she would have seen.

Tessa bit her lip. "Sorry, that was insensitive. All I'm saying is that maybe you should take a break from the idea of romance and just have some fun instead. You knew what you were getting into with him when you started, but somewhere along the way you forgot. Let's go back to the old Lily, the one that was just in it for the fun." Tessa disappeared into the bathroom for a moment, leaving Lily to decide whether she was really up for going out or not. When Tessa came back she no longer had the curling iron, and her hair was all done in perfect loose curls. She immediately started mussing them with her fingers to give them a bit of a wild look. It made all the difference, turning her from good girl to sex goddess. The blond looked good with the dark lipstick she was wearing.

 Lily had a feeling her friend would not be coming back to the apartment tonight.

"Well, we're going out for drinks at least," Tessa said continuing to pick apart her curls. "And after that we'll see how you feel. But please, please take a shower before we go because you smell like a bread factory." She walked past Lily into the kitchen, gesturing like a game show host towards the bathroom door.

Lily sighed and went into the bathroom. It might do her some good to get out for a while.

* * *

The club was a small, cramped space with a narrow staircase leading down from the sign outside to a heavy black door plastered with peeling posters advertising upcoming DJ events. Inside was a darkly-lit bar counter, a couple of sofas, and a few sparse tables.

People milled about either sipping on drinks or taking a break from the chaos in the other room. The deep bass beat rattled the building to its foundations, and Lily felt herself wondering how people in the nearby apartment buildings managed to get any sleep.
Lily was content to sit in the relative quiet of the bar and people watch, but Tessa as always, was itching to go onto the dance floor.

"Let's get our drinks and go in," she said, tugging Lily towards the bar counter. "I'm not going to let you mope around by yourself."

Tessa got the attention of the bartender who was busy polishing glasses. He was a young, well-built man with a ponytail. He waved them away saying, "We're not using this bar tonight. You'll have to go inside to get drinks." He gestured with the glass he was holding towards the next room.

Tessa pulled Lily away from the bar. "I guess you don't have a choice," she said, looking far happier than Lily would have liked.

Tessa always seemed to get her way, either through brute persistence or some strange twist of fate, like tonight. Lily sighed and followed her friend into the wall of moving bodies in the other room.

The crowd jostled Lily as they made their way across the room to the long bar counter at the other end. The space was larger than Lily had imagined, but still uncomfortably packed for Lily's current headspace. She just wanted to sit and drink and forget everything that had happened in the past few months.

Tessa ordered two shots as Lily sat down at the bar. She slid one over to Lily who promptly slid it back. Tessa shrugged her shoulders and downed both, one after another like a pro.

"You know where to find me," she said, letting herself be sucked in by the crowd until her blond hair was out of sight.

Lily turned and ordered a drink of her own, something with gin in it that sounded sweet. If she needed to, she would return to the shots later.

A man sat down next to her and ordered a drink. He was wearing skinny black jeans that emphasized his thin frame and a black t-shirt with the sleeves cut off. Lily noticed a scar down his face, but besides that he had nice features. At least, nice enough for the club they were at. He brushed his longish hair away from his forehead and smiled at her.

"Tired of dancing?" he asked.

"I haven't even started," Lily replied. "I'm not really feeling it today."

The man laughed. "Yeah, I saw the friend you were with earlier. I'm guessing she's the one that dragged you here."

"You've been watching me?" Lily asked with a raised eyebrow. She wasn't exactly flirting, but she wasn't not flirting either. This man was a nice distraction from the negative thoughts swirling in her head, however briefly.

The man held up his hands. "No, I just happened to see you and remembered you. It's hard not to remember a girl like you. Hey, let me get you something to drink."

Lily looked down at her still half-full glass. "No thanks," she said. She did not want to feel like she owed the man anything, or encourage him to stick around longer than she liked.

"Okay, no problem." The man rested his hands on the bar counter while he waited for his drink. They were thin, almost delicate, a contrast to Evan's strong hands whose touch Lily still yearned for despite her feelings of anger towards him.

There was just something about Evan that was like a magnet, pulling her towards him though her mind told her to stay away. Even now, after all he had done to her, she still felt herself thinking about him all the time.

"Hey, you're not seeing anyone, are you?" the man asked suddenly. "I mean, I wouldn't want to be unpleasantly surprised when your boyfriend comes out of the crowd to beat the shit out of me. It wouldn't be the first time I've been on the wrong end of a misunderstanding." He tapped the scar on his face, his humble smile disarming.

Lily smiled back.

"No," she replied, pushing away thoughts of Evan, "I'm not seeing anyone. But I'm not really looking either."

"Fair enough," the man said.

At that moment, Tessa pushed herself through the crowd and took the open stool next to Lily. Lily turned away from the man to talk to her friend, whose face was bright and sweaty from dancing.

"You should get out there!" she yelled, much louder than was necessary to be heard over the music. "This place is amazing. We should have come here from the start. I'm never going back to those overpriced clubs in Hollywood. The people here are insane. Okay, I'm going."

Tessa leaped off her stool and disappeared back into the crowd before Lily could even get a word in. She was glad at least one of them was having fun.

"I bought you that drink anyway," the man said almost apologetically when Lily turned back around. Lily offered an insincere smile of thanks, wondering how long the guy was planning to stick around. She had already made it clear she wasn't interested in starting anything tonight.

She quietly sipped at her first drink, making it last so she didn't have to accept the one he had bought her. The ice was starting to water down the cocktail, making it bitter.

"See you around, maybe?" the man said as he left the bar.

Lily was glad to see the back of him, but at the same time she had enjoyed the company. Drinking alone at the bar was doing nothing for her self-esteem.

She finished her drink, leaving the one the man had bought for her untouched, and pushed herself into the mass of heaving bodies. She listened to the music and watched the people around her dancing with reckless abandon. Eventually, she too lost herself in the crowd. Her stress melted away as she moved with the people around her, never staying long with one partner but feeling for once not alone.

After a couple of dances, she was starting to feel exhausted. Her movements dragged and her eyelids fluttered. At first, she thought it was the stress of the week finally catching up to her, but then Evan's words from that night came back to her in a flash. She had been drugged.

She stumbled through the crowd, frantically searching for Tessa before her body succumbed to sleep. The man from the bar appeared by her side and offered a hand to stabilize her.

"Let's get you out of here," he said.

Lily clumsily pushed him off her, her instinct for danger kicking in. She tumbled backwards into the crowd and a man with braids in his hair caught her just as she was about to tumble to the floor.

"Are you okay?" the man asked her.

"I need to find my friend," Lily shouted, her words slurring together. "I need her to take me home."

A woman appeared out of nowhere and started shouting questions at Lily over the pounding music. "What's your friend's name? What does she look like?"

Lily's knees buckled.

"Lily!" Tessa's waves of blond hair appeared through the crowd and she was soon at her friend's side.

Lily leaned on her. "I need to get out of here." Her legs felt like jelly and the floor was spinning up towards her. A firm hand pulled her back upright.

"Hey, your friend doesn't look too good. Do you live near here? We'll help get her outside."

The man's voice sounded like it was coming from underwater. All Lily could see was the rainbow flashing of lights in the club and was only barely aware of the bodies pressing against her as she was half-dragged out of the building and onto the sidewalk outside.

The next thing Lily remembered was waking up in her bed the next morning with a pounding headache and a mouth dry as sandpaper.

She rolled over groaning and found the glass of water and aspirin pills Tessa had left for her on the nightstand. She popped the pills into her mouth and swallowed them, chugging the entire glass of water down with them.

She lay back down, trying to recall what she could of that night. She had gone to the club with Tessa, and that man had bought her a drink. No, she never drank the one he bought her. He must have slipped something into hers when she wasn't looking. But she had been sitting at the bar the entire time. She tried to picture what the man looked like so she could describe him to the police.

Tall, thin, probably about Lily's own age with a scar on his face and a weaselly look in his eyes she hadn't liked. Of course, that could just be her impression now knowing what he had tried to do to her. Lily was sick to think that at the time, she had kind of liked him.

Her first instinct was to call Evan and tell him what happened, but then she remembered their fight. She set her phone back down on the nightstand and pulled the covers up over her head. She promised herself to stay away from men for a while. They were nothing but trouble.

* * *

The apartment building looked the same as any of the other abandoned buildings on the street, at least from the outside. On the inside, it was a hollow shell. The company who owned the lot had gone bankrupt before they could even finish the building, leaving it gutted on the inside with the metal scaffolding and concrete floors lying bare.

Its windows were boarded up, never having been fitted with glass in the first place. The front door hung crooked on its hinges and graffiti splashed the few walls that had been completed inside.

Evan's boots echoed against the cold concrete, their sound bouncing up through the structure and announcing his arrival to anyone waiting there. He was to go down to the basement parking garage, but he worried he wouldn't even make it that far.

He knew from experience that Al was not above stabbing someone in the back, and he doubted Darien was any different. Evan's scar tingled with foreboding. If Darien had planned to jump him before he could get downstairs, Evan was a perfect target. There were too many places to hide up here, and sound carried far.

But Evan made it to the staircase without incident. The door had been propped open and Evan could hear loud voices coming up from the garage, along with a few roars. Evan crossed the wide, empty floor of the parking garage toward the group of men and lions gathered at the other end. Half he recognized from his own pride, the others from Darien's. Al was there taking bets, slinking among the men like a weasel and pocketing their money as he scribbled in his ledger. Evan didn't want to know what the odds were on him. Darien had not shown up yet.

A short, wrinkled man with a scar across his nose waved at Evan. He was a good friend of Evan's father and one of the oldest lions in the pride. He made a show of placing his bet with Al, waving a hundred-dollar bill and saying Evan's name loudly enough for him to hear. Al shrugged his shoulders as he took the bet, probably thinking the man was about to lose a lot of money.

"Evan," the man said in his gruff but friendly voice. "I thought you'd come with your father. And Matt, where's Matt?"

Evan had purposely not told his family that he was challenging Darien for Lily tonight. The only reason he had asked the others to come was because he needed the muscle in case Darien decided to play dirty, or refused to accept the outcome. Lions usually regarded the results of a fight as the final say, but every once in a while, there was a bad loser who had to be subdued by force.

The members of Darien's pride who had volunteered to keep the peace had already transformed and were pacing the parking garage, five hundred pounds of lean muscle with sharp claws and a powerful

169

bite. It was a terrifying sight to anyone not used to it, though Evan, too, felt a little apprehension watching the lions pace.

He didn't want to think of what would happen if those lions had to lay down the law tonight. He hoped that Darien would accept defeat gracefully. Or, if Evan lost, that Darien would not go in for the kill.

"The fight's going to start soon. You'd better get ready." The old man patted Evan on the back.

The crowd formed into a ring as Evan pulled off his shirt. He had not seen Darien yet, and was feeling apprehensive. The fight was supposed to start any minute now, and his challenger was still not here. Evan unbuckled his belt.

The door to the staircase banged open and a roar thundered through the concrete parking garage. One of the largest lions Evan had ever seen came slinking out of the shadow of the doorway. The outer ring of its mane was a dark brown, contrasting sharply with the golden fur around its face and down its back. Its fangs shone menacingly as his jowls drew back to let out a series of deep growls.

Evan steeled himself for the coming fight, knowing he could not afford to hold back. It was going to be a fight to the death. As the crowd parted to let Darien enter the ring, Evan stepped out of his jeans and tossed them out of the way.

He rolled his neck and stretched his arms out behind him, letting the power of his animal form consume his body. Fur grew over his lengthening body as his face grew into jaws and teeth. A roar rumbled up from deep inside his belly as the final remnants of his human form succumbed to the beast inside.

When the transformation was complete, he stood at equal height with Darien. His tufted tail curled up behind him, poised for battle as the rest of him. The ring of spectators fell silent as Evan and Darien faced one another, neither moving a muscle as they waited for the other to make the first move.

Evan's tail twitched and Darien came at him. His massive paws swiped at Evan's face, their claws just barely missing the flesh through the thickness of Evan's mane. He backed up and roared at Darien, warning him against a second attack.

It was now Evan's turn to take the offensive. Still growling, he advanced on Darien. Darien tried to back up out of the way but was stopped by the wall of lions and men blocking his retreat behind him. Evan pummeled his face with his paws, not yet using his claws as he wanted Darien to surrender if he could without drawing blood. Darien lunged back, his jaws aiming for the side of Evan's neck. It was a sign that Darien would not offer Evan the same mercy.

Evan pushed him away and their bodies smashed against one another, each trying to get their teeth around the other's neck. Evan swatted at Darien's snout, his claw raking a gash that dripped blood into Evan's mane as the two continued to go at each other. Evan reared on his hind legs and came down on his opponent from above, hoping to pin the lion down onto the ground and force him to surrender.

But Darien shoved Evan to the side and he lost his balance. He twisted towards the floor and landed on his back. Darien went for Evan's neck, biting and slashing as Evan fought to keep him off. Finally, he maneuvered out from under Darien and got to his feet, narrowly missing a fatal bite.

A burning in Evan's side told him he had been scratched. He shook it off and doubled his resolve. Lily was all that mattered. He was doing this for her.

Evan lunged at Darien again, this time forcing the other lion onto the ground. Darien clamped his jaws around Evan's foreleg and Evan roared out in pain. He could feel the immense power of Darien's jaws working to crush the bones in his leg. He sank his claws into Darien's side and wrenched himself away.

His leg felt like it was on fire and it wouldn't hold his weight. His leg buckled and his head hit the concrete. Darien held him down, his claws sinking in to Evan's shoulder. Darien opened his jaws and let out a roar of triumph. All Evan could see above him were the teeth that would soon be around his throat.

Evan knew in that moment that this was the end.

CHAPTER NINE

The first gunshots rang out at 11:00pm on the quiet residential street in South Los Angeles. It took a moment before those inside the house realized what was happening, but by then it was too late. One of the boys lay in a slowly growing puddle of his own blood, with the sinking feeling in his gut that he wasn't the only one who had been hit.

His thigh burned where the 9mm bullet from a semiautomatic handgun had pierced through the front window of his parents' home and lodged in the muscle. Every beat of his heart sent a fresh wave of blood onto the beige carpet.

His mother, crawling along the floor to avoid any more gunfire, clutched her cell phone and called 911 as she cried for her injured son. She too had been hit, but only grazed in the arm. Her concern was for her son. She told the other one to hide in the bathroom, in case the gunmen came back.

On the third floor of a government housing project downtown, a similar scene played out. A father lay with a kitchen towel wrapped around his arm, the white cloth slowly turning to crimson. He had been taking out the trash when the car drove by. He only saw the

flash of gunpowder and felt the searing pain in his bicep. He had
been lucky to have been hit only once.

The bullets had sprayed the pavement in front of him, and he had
only escaped by hiding behind the dumpster. After the car had gone,
he ran upstairs to check on his family and get something to stop the
bleeding. His wife and daughter fussed over him while they waited
for a ride to the hospital.

And on another street in another neighborhood, more members of
Evan's pride were reeling after their own close-calls with death. In
all, three houses had been hit with two injuries and no fatalities.
Darien's pride had hit hard, and now Evan's was in a state of chaos.

Evan's father had taken up his old role as leader of the pride until
his son could be contacted to come help. As he drove to the hospital
to see how the injured members of his pride were doing, he called
his son. But no matter how many times Evan's phone rang, his son
did not pick up.

* * *

It was late when the man knocked on her door. Lily didn't bother to
look at the time, but Tessa was already asleep and Lily had no
intention of leaving the comfort of her place on the sofa to go see

who was knocking on her door at such a late hour. The man knocked again, then a muffled voice came in through the door.

"Excuse me, but I think your car's being towed."

Lily sat up and rushed to the door. She opened it while keeping the chain locked. Looking out through the crack of the door she could see one of her neighbors standing there. He smiled when he saw her.

"I'm sorry to bother you at such a late hour, but I was going out for cigarettes and I saw a car being towed and recognized it as yours. You always park down on San Marino, right? The maroon Volvo?"

Lily swore. It was definitely her car. "Thanks, I'll go check it out," she said and closed the door.

She had no idea why it was being towed, but she couldn't afford to be without a car or even pay the towing fee. She had to see if she could stop them from taking it.
She unhooked the chain and ran downstairs. She jogged the few blocks to where she always parked her car but it was right where she left it and there was no tow truck to be seen.

Lily's shoulders sagged with relief. Had there been another maroon Volvo parked on the same street that had been towed? It seemed unlikely, but there was no other explanation. While she was checking her windshield for a parking ticket, a hand closed over her mouth and the cold steel of a gun pressed into her back.

"Don't scream or I shoot," a low voice said into her ear. Lily whimpered in fear, the sounds strangled by the hand over her mouth. "I said, not a sound."

Lily was dragged backwards and shoved into the backseat of her own car. The man pointing the gun at her got in beside her and she got a good look at his face. He was pudgy with a weak chin, but the deep set of his eyes gave him a threatening appearance. He kept the gun trained on Lily as another man got into the front seat. She could only see his back, and his green eyes in the rearview mirror.

"There's someone who wants to see you," he said.

The phone call had saved his life. It was a miracle that his father's friend had heard his phone buzzing in the pocket of Evan's discarded jeans over the sounds of the fight and the shouts of the men watching. But as soon as the man had heard the pride had been attacked, he had sent the other lions in to intervene before Darien could go in for the kill.

They wrestled the furious Darien to the ground while Evan shifted back to ask the men what had happened. Apparently, his pride had been the victims of a series of drive-by shootings. There had been thankfully no fatalities, but it was pretty clear who was behind the attacks.

The few who knew about the phone call kept the real reason for stopping the fight a secret from the others, allowing Evan and the others to leave the parking garage without it turning into an all-out brawl. Evan would have to bide his time if he wanted retribution.

Evan's arm throbbed as he drove to the hospital. The bandages he had wrapped around it were already damp with blood, but he rolled his sleeve down to hide it. He couldn't have the others worrying about him, not now. As the alpha of the pride, he had to stay strong for them no matter what.

At the hospital, Evan went straight to the third floor, intensive care. He asked the woman in green scrubs at the nurse's station which rooms his friends were in.

"Let me check, one second," she said as she flipped through a stack of papers clamped to a clipboard on her desk.

As she searched, a small red light lit up on a panel by her side along with a low, steady beeping.

"Could you hold on for a second?" she asked Evan. "I need to check on a patient."

She left the nurses' station while Evan was standing there, wondering if the members of his pride were okay.

After she was gone, Evan took the clipboard she had been looking at from the desk and scanned the names. Bill, one of the men Evan's father had grown up with, had his name on the list next to the room number 202 and on the same floor was Jack, Evan's kid cousin who he barely even remembered. It had been a long time since the whole pride had been together, and Evan couldn't recall just how many there were.

He realized he had failed them and he promised himself he would do everything he could to make things right. For now, he was glad that neither of them were on the third floor.

Chester's room was closest to the elevator doors so Evan went there first.

The man's upper arm was bandaged tightly and his family sat around him talking. His wife looked exhausted but happy, and his young daughter sat half on the bed, laughing and making jokes. His son, sitting a little apart from the rest but nonetheless involved in the conversation, was maybe ten years younger than Evan, still in high school but just as tall and almost as strong.

If he wasn't careful, the kid might challenge him to become alpha before his own cubs could. The thought of children brought a fresh pang of pain to Evan's chest that he tried to ignore.

"How are you feeling?" he asked the grizzled man.

"Oh, this?" Chester replied, raising his arm and wincing. He lowered it back onto the bed. "I've had far worse done to me in my youth than any gun could do to me now. You know how strong a lion's jaws are."

Evan's dad loved telling the story of how Chester had gotten into a fight with a transient shifter causing trouble in the city, and how the beast had clamped down on Chester's hand and crushed most of the bones in it. He still had trouble gripping things with that hand. It was good to see that the years hadn't taken any of the toughness from him.

"But what about you?" the man asked. "It looks like you should be in here instead of me."

Evan put a hand to his temple where it was the most tender and his fingers came away sticky with blood. He wiped them on his jeans. "I was being stupid and got into a fight. I should have been there for you guys. I'm sorry."

"You couldn't have known they would do this. None of us did." The man shook his head.

"I just wish we knew why they did it," his wife said, grasping her husband's hand. "There was no warning, and no explanation. We only assume it was the other pride because, well, who else would do something like this? Three families from our pride, and in three separate neighborhoods. This wasn't random."

Chester squeezed his wife's hand. "Whatever it is, I'm sure we'll figure it out. But for now we've got to just be glad no one was killed." Then to Evan, "Let me know what you find out, okay? There's a rumor going around that it has something to do with your brother. But I'm not willing to believe it just yet. Whoever brought this down on us is going to have hell to pay for it."

Evan nodded and went out into the hallway. He couldn't help thinking that he was the one who had caused this. He didn't know why, but somehow, he was responsible. But what was it supposed to have achieved, attacking his friends and family while he was busy fighting Darien?

Had he lost the fight it would have made no sense. It would have been a pointless risk. It would have made more sense to wait to see the outcome of the fight before going out and trying to gun down three families.

Evan wandered down the hall, realizing that he couldn't quite remember what room his cousin was in. It was either 212 or 214, but it would be easy enough to find either way. He could see the doors to both rooms open down the hall, and ducked into 212 to see if Jack was there.

Instead, hooked up to tubes and looking like something out of a wax museum, was the true alpha of Darien's pride lying quietly on the bed. Youssef opened his eyes at the sound of Evan entering the room. Before he could duck back out, Youssef spoke.

"I'm sorry for what has happened to your pride. I heard about the attacks, and I want you to know that I didn't order them."

"Then who did?" Evan asked, finding himself sitting down next to the old man's bed.

Youssef sighed. "I know what you're thinking, but it wasn't Darien. He can be arrogant and he's prone to taking risks, but he would never do something like this. No, this was someone else."

"But why did they do it?" Evan asked, feeling way out of his depth. Youssef was a true alpha. Evan had no right being the pillar of his own pride. He lacked the experience, the wisdom. He wished his father was here to tell him what to do.

Youssef coughed. "I heard there's a woman in the city who has the scent. Whoever did this wants the same thing you do. To make her his mate."

"But you said it wasn't Darien. And besides, I was challenging him for the woman when the attacks happened. We never finished the fight. I doubt he would do something so drastic when he still had a chance of winning."

"Is Darien the only young man in our pride?"

Evan recalled his talk with Al. Though at the time the man had had no interest in helping Evan against Darien, there had still been the gleam of ambition in his eyes when Evan had talked of Al becoming alpha. Was Al the one behind all of this? Did he want Lily, too?

"And the girl, you have to find the poor girl," Youssef said with urgency, as if suddenly remembering the most important point.

"Lily?" Evan asked.

"If that's her name, then yes. You said the fight was interrupted when you came here. Darien will take that as a forfeit. He'll go after the girl. You need to go find her now and make sure she's not in danger."

"Why are you helping me?" Evan asked.

Youssef had always been the one voice of reason at the head of his otherwise unruly pride. But to go so far as to help his son's rival seemed too out of character. Blood ran deep within prides, and to sell out your own no matter the situation was never a decision taken lightly.

Lions were social animals. They needed their pride, and the pride needed them. A fractured pride would not last long.

"Because," the man said, his eyes closing momentarily as if he were trying to reserve strength. "I raised Darien. He is a smart boy, ruthless, and never takes no for an answer. These traits are what make him so good at the business we do, but they don't make him a good man. I worry about the girl and what he may do to her. There is too much animal in him and too little humanity. He's a predator and he'll devour her until there's nothing left."

A cold chill ran through Evan's body as he imagined Darien going after Lily. He may even be with her right now. Evan had to find her as soon as he could. He had to protect her.

"Thank you," he said to the man on the bed. "And I'm sorry for what I might have to do."

"I've already accepted the end of my reign. It's time for another family to take my place." Youssef's eyes closed. Evan left him to rest.

Evan decided he would visit Jack another time. Right now he had to find Lily. He ran out of the hospital and got in his car, heading straight for Lily's apartment. As he drove he dialed her number. She didn't pick up, meaning either she was asleep or already in trouble. Evan prayed it was the former. He sped through the streets of downtown LA, the buildings and palm trees lining the streets going by in a blur as he pushed the limits of his speedometer. The light ahead turned red and he slammed on the brakes cursing loudly.

His car skidded to a stop just before the intersection. He pounded on the steering wheel in frustration and fresh pain shot up his injured arm causing him to curse again.

As soon as the light was green Evan floored it. He made it to Lily's apartment in good time and ran up the steps to her door. Tessa opened at his knock, looking like she had just been sleeping. Her hair flew out in all directions and an eye mask was pulled high her forehead.

"What the hell do you want?" she grumbled out at him. The chain lock kept the door mostly closed so he couldn't see past her into the apartment.

"Is Lily here?" Evan asked.

Tessa's face scrunched into a scowl. "She doesn't want to see you."

"But is she here?" Evan tried to control the agitation in his voice.

"Why wouldn't she be? It's after midnight. You probably woke her up with all your banging and yelling at our door."

"But can you just check?" Evan asked. He didn't care if she didn't want to talk to him, but he needed to be sure she was safe.

Tessa rolled her eyes. "Fine, give me a second." The door closed, but through it he could hear Tessa calling Lily's name.

"Hey, Evan's here. He wants to talk to you or something. I dunno. He's being a real pain in the—"

Tessa voice trailed away and the door opened, all the way this time. "She's not here," Tessa said, panic in her voice. "She was here when I went to sleep. Let me call her cell."
The phone rang, but no answer.

"Shit," Evan said. He knew who had her. "I'm going to find Lily. You stay here in case she comes back or anyone else shows up to the apartment. I think I know where she is, and she might be in danger. Has anyone come by the apartment lately?"

"She had a few guys following her for a while, but they haven't bothered her recently. But if Lily's in any sort of trouble I should go with you. She's my best friend and I owe it to her."

Evan looked at the small woman standing in the doorway in her pink pajama shorts and matching top. He doubted she would be able to help him much, and worried about having to look after her if she went with him.

He rubbed his neck where a knot had formed. "I really don't think—"

"Give me two minutes," Tessa said.

She disappeared into the apartment, and when she came back she was wearing what could only have been described as combat gear. Knee high boots covered her previously bare feet and a leather jacket covered her pink tank top. She pulled a 9mm from a holster on her hip.

Evan had to admit even he was a little scared. "Where did you get that gun?"

Tessa put the gun back in its holster. "These streets can be dangerous for a young woman all alone. I like to stay prepared."

Evan shook his head in disbelief. "Yeah, I guess you can come with me. But please tell me you know how to handle that thing."

Tessa smiled. "I go to the shooting range every week."

* * *

The duct tape around Lily's wrists was cutting off her circulation. She clenched her hands to try to get the blood flowing again. Tears fell from her eyes and ran down the duct tape across her mouth. Her breaths came out ragged as she shook in fear. Two men stood at the door of the apartment while a third sat next to her on the sofa. She tried to wriggle away from his touch, but there was nowhere for her to go.

"There's no need to be afraid," the man said.

Though Lily had never seen the two men at the door before, she recognized him as the man from the club—the man who had drugged her. His name was Al. Or, at least that's what the other two men called him.

His hand rested on her knee, its touch soft but menacing. "We're giving you a choice. It's up to you."

But Lily knew it wasn't up to her. She had to give in to this man's demands, or he would take everything from her. She shook her head.

"Is that a no?"

She had no idea what they had planned for her if she refused, but she had a clear enough picture of what they were expecting her to agree to. This man, Al, was a shifter like Evan. And for some reason, all the shifters were after her. They all wanted her for their mate, and the one who succeeded would be considered the most dominant among them. Evan had been no different than the rest, apparently.

While she had thought he found her attractive and maybe even loved her, he was really just pursuing her out of the primal instinct inside of him. And where was he now, when she most needed him?

Al wanted her to agree to become his mate, or he would destroy her life.

Just when Lily thought things could not get any worse, the apartment door opened and Darien walked in.

"What the fuck is this?" he asked, rushing Al and grabbing him by the collar. Al fought to get away but he was no match for the much stronger man.

"Darien, I didn't expect, this isn't—"

Darien twisted Al's collar in his grip so that the fabric cut off Al's breathing. Al choked and sputtered in Darien's face.

"You backstabbing bastard. Did you think you could undermine me and take the girl for yourself?"

Al's fingers grasped desperately at Darien's. He looked like he would not last much longer. Darien shook him and threw him to the ground. Al looked up at him with true fear in his eyes.

"You thought you could pull one over on us. You thought you could take the girl while no one was looking, while Evan and I were too busy fighting each other. And you planned the attack on Evan's pride to buy yourself even more time.

"But it didn't work. I caught on to your scheme. I'm the alpha, not you, and as soon as I have the girl, I'll be the leader of the most powerful pride in all of California. I'll rule the streets of this city, and the first thing I'll do is kick the scum like you out."

"Please, give me a chance," Al pleaded, groveling pathetically at Darien's feet. "I can earn my place back in the pride, I promise. You can have the girl. I'll help you."

Darien looked at the man cowering at his feet with disgust. "Get up." Then to Lily, "I'm sorry it came down to this."

He went over to her and knelt down in front of her. His hand went to her face and she flinched. He pulled the tape off her mouth, then kissed her aching lips. She wrenched away and spit in his face.

"Let me go, you bastard!" she shouted.

One of the men at the door put his finger to his lips then moved it across his throat in a slitting gesture. Lily got the message. She stopped yelling.

Darien brushed back her wavy hair with his hand, the strands damp with sweat and tears.
"So, what is it Al has planned for you?" he asked in a sickeningly sweet tone.

"She has to decide," Al said. "She has to accept you as her mate, or we drug her up and leave her somewhere out in the desert where either the cops find her or she dies trying to make her way back. She wants to be a Hollywood star, like that piece of shit Evan. All we

191

have to do is ruin her reputation and she'll never be able to work again. Evan won't want her after that, I'm sure.

You know how hard he's worked to bury his past, his brother's drug problems and time in jail. There's no way he'd come to her defense. And if she dies out there, well," he gave Lily an apologetic shrug.

Lily started sobbing, her fear threatening to send her into shock. These men were not intending to let her go no matter what she did. But she could at least keep her dignity, the little she had left. In the back of her mind, she prayed that Evan would somehow find her, and rescue her from this horrible nightmare before she condemned herself to death.

CHAPTER TEN

"I'd die before I let you touch me," Lily spat.

"Maybe you'd like to reconsider that answer," Darien said with threat in his eyes.

"Go fuck yourself," Lily shouted.

She didn't care any more. She was angry and disgusted with these men and there was nothing left for her to care about. Her fear had left her as soon as she had accepted this. She wanted them to feel the rage boiling in her blood.

Darien smacked her across the face with the back of his hand. He signaled to the two men at the door and they came towards her. One cut the duct tape around her wrists while Al prepared a syringe. Lily kicked and fought the men holding her down as Al handed the syringe to Darien.

"It's not the usual stuff. It's gonna mess her up really bad. We've gotta get her out into the desert before she starts hallucinating, or she might get violent."

Lily screamed at the top of her lungs, but a thick hand around her windpipe cut it off. She could feel a rubber tube being pulled tight across her upper arm and the icy coldness of something inside her elbow, then the stab of the needle as it pierced her skin. She stopped struggling, knowing she would only hurt herself if she fought now.

As the chemicals entered her blood stream, her pupils dilated and the muscles in her arm twitched. A bead of tainted blood remained on her skin as Darien removed the needle. The man holding her arm pulled the tube loose and rubbed her arm. She could already feel the drugs surging through her body.

"Tie her back up," Darien said, then walked into a back room.

One of the men roughly grabbed Lily's arms behind her back and wound her wrists with more duct tape. Her ankles were still bound from before, though she had tried countless times to kick herself free.

Lily leaned weakly against the back of the sofa. She closed her eyes, tears escaping through her closed lashes as she regretted everything that had brought her to this moment. From what the men had said, it seemed that once Lily had chosen a mate the bond had to be honored no matter what.

In Lily's opinion, she had already chosen Evan. They had already been intimate, and he was the only one who had not come after her by force. She had chosen to sleep with him, to spend time with him, and to even let herself fall in love. Though she hadn't replied on the night of the argument when he had told her he loved her, her feelings had been the same as his. She loved him.

But now it didn't matter, because she was going to be driven out into the desert and abandoned. These drugs that were coursing through her system were already making her lose sense of time. How long had she been sitting on the sofa since the needle left her arm? Her eyes opened and closed sleepily and she slumped sideways, not caring if she fell asleep in her last moments of peace.

An arm roughly jerked her up and another wrapped around her waist. They were taking her somewhere, but she didn't want to go. She wanted to stay on the sofa and sleep, letting the drugs do their thing while she dreamed until morning.

Someone kicked her legs to make her go faster, but her legs were bound together and she couldn't move. One of the men hoisted her over his shoulder and carried her down the stairs to the van waiting outside. He chucked her in the back and slammed the sliding door. Inside the van was dark and smelled like cigarette smoke. Lily rolled on to her side to take the pressure off her aching arms bound behind her back.

Lily could see streaks of light passing the windows as the van left the city. They looked like shooting stars, but in a rainbow of colors that made Lily think of Ferris wheel lights. Lily always liked the circus, but hadn't been since she was a child. As she recalled the memories, she could smell the cotton candy and the tinkling music of the carousel as its painted animals went around and around in endless circles.

Just thinking about them made Lily dizzy. She liked the big top, too, and the circus shows with clowns and dancing bears and the lion tamer. Lily didn't like thinking about the lions, though. Something deep in her brain sent out alarm signals as she thought of their wide jaws opening and the lion tamer sticking his head in to show the audience how brave he was.

But it wasn't brave, it was stupid. Lions were savage beasts that could not be tamed, could not be predicted. And even if you thought a lion loved you, you were really only their prey. Lily had been Evan's prey, but he had left her for something better.

The van bumped and jolted as it left the paved roads and turned onto a dirt path. They had left the city lights and skyscrapers and were now headed through the dusty desert landscape on the outskirts of the city, the wide expanse of tan like the color of a lion's fur dotted by short bush scrubs and gnarled trees. In the dark it was pitch black, no light to reach it but the stars splashed above and the narrow crescent moon, which offered little more than a faint glow.

Lily felt like she had been in the van forever. The men were mostly silent, though every once in a while, they spoke in what sounded to Lily like an alien tongue. She was starting to forget what words sounded like, and though she tried to call out to her kidnappers her own words came out garbled and incoherent.

Eventually, the van slowed and stopped, and the wide back door opened to give Lily her first real glimpse of the desert. The air was cool, almost cold, and Lily shivered in her shorts and tank top. One of the men cut the tape around her wrists and ankles and told her to get out of the van. Her movements were jittery and weak, and when she failed to follow orders fast enough a rough hand smacked her on the rump.

"Hurry the fuck up," the man growled.

Lily did as she was told and stood at the back of the van, her arms around herself to try to stop the shivering.

She couldn't remember who the men were, or what she was doing there. "Please, I need to go home," she said, her voice weak and cracking.

The man laughed. "This is your new home. You get to live with the rattlesnakes."

Lily whimpered and clutched the man's arm. "I don't want to stay here. Take me home, please."

The man put his arm around her. Lily thought the gesture was to comfort her, but he was actually pushing her away from the van. When she was far enough away, he turned back and slammed the van door shut.

"Stay there," he said as he walked around to the driver's seat.

The taillights flashed bright red, nearly blinding Lily who stood dazed in their crimson light. She held her hands in front of her eyes to shield them.

The van sped away, leaving Lily coughing in a cloud of dust and blinking away the afterimages of the car's taillights bouncing across her vision. She was all alone, with no sense of direction. She could not even see the distant lights of civilization to tell her which way to go. For a second she thought she saw a circus tent and Ferris wheel in the distance, but when she blinked, the image vanished again.

Dazed out of her mind as the drugs continued to play tricks with her perception, Lily stumbled after the tracks the van's tires had left in the dirt. It was hard to keep following them, and her bare feet ached as she tripped over rocks and other things she couldn't see in the pitch-black night. She was sure the soles of her feet were bleeding, leaving a damp red trail of her progress through the desert.

Eventually she gave up, having lost the trail of the van and too tired to go on. She dropped to the ground in frustration and hugged her knees to herself. It seemed stupid, but the one person she really wanted to see right then was Evan, even after everything that had happened. She would have given anything to have his big dumb arms around her and his deep voice in her ear telling her everything would be okay.

Lily rocked back and forth, sobbing silently as she waited for dawn to come. She didn't know if there really were rattlesnakes in the desert like the man had said, or other things that might hurt her. The darkness was heavy around her, the moon far too dim. She started to feel nauseous and sweat dripped down her back making her colder than she already was. If this was the end, she wanted it to come soon.

* * *

Evan had exhausted every hideaway, every drug den and safe house in the city, but there were no signs of either Al or Darien. The members of their pride he had met had not known anything about

199

Lily, not even when questioned under threat of grave injury. He had to find someone closer to them, if he could not find the men themselves.

Tessa sat next to him in the car, tapping her fingers against the dashboard in front of her. She was keyed up from all of the interrogations and wouldn't stop talking. "Maybe we can go back to that old man, the one in the hospital you mentioned. Put some pressure on him and get him to talk."

"It's no use," Evan sighed. "He's the one who told me find Lily. If he had known where she was, he would have mentioned it. There has to be somewhere I'm not thinking of."

"Wait a second!" Tessa shouted.

Evan nearly drove off the road in alarm.

"What?" he asked angrily once his heartbeat had resumed its normal pace.

"The guy who drugged Lily."

Evan almost ran off the road a second time.

"Yeah," Tessa said, nodding her head. "We went to this club in the neighborhood and the guy must've slipped something into her drink. I got her home and took care of her, but the guy might have something to do with all this."

"Why didn't you say something earlier?" Evan asked accusingly. He tried to temper the anger in his voice, reminding himself that Tessa was not the one to blame here. "I'm sorry. What did the guy look like?"

"He was thin, younger than you but probably not by much. He had kinda long brown hair and a scar on his face right here." Evan glanced over as Tessa traced a line down her cheek. "Yeah, that scar was pretty noticeable."

Evan turned at the next signal, doubling back into Koreatown. He thought he had exhausted all of the possibilities, but there might be someone at the club who knew Al.

"Can you tell me how to get there?"

"Yeah," Tessa replied. "It's about five blocks from our place. You just turn on the street with the church instead of going straight."

Evan allowed himself a small feeling of hope. "You know, I could kiss you," he said.

Tessa replied, "Isn't that what got you in trouble with Lily in the first place? How about you save those kisses for her when we rescue her."

Evan laughed in spite of the situation. Something told him he was on the right track, as if that magnetism that had drawn him to Lily was now leading him straight for her. But a pang of guilt soon overshadowed his optimism. If Al was truly the one behind all of this, it was Evan's fault for planting that seed of ambition in Al's mind.

He had gotten Al to see the possibility of becoming alpha and apparently, Al had taken it to heart. The man was trying to steal Lily from both Evan and Darien, though he was no match for either of them in strength. He knew that if he had the girl, none of the rest mattered.

Evan could feel the bass in his bones before he even stepped foot in the club. It rose up from the basement through the concrete and into the neighboring buildings rattling them from foundation to roof. He pushed open the heavy door and was met by a rush of sound as the music blasted his ears in full force. He elbowed past the crowd jamming up the doorway and went to talk to the bartender.

"You know Al?" he said.

The ponytailed man looked at him suspiciously. "Depends on who you are." And then to Tessa in a much lighter tone, "Hey, didn't I see you here the other night?"

"Yeah, the night Al drugged my friend and tried to take advantage of her." Tessa's glare could have pierced bulletproof glass.

The bartender shook his head. "He may be a piece of shit, but he's not that kind of guy."

"So, you do know him." Evan said, crossing his arms over his chest.

The bartender looked guiltily away from him.

"No, I mean—" the man was backing away from the bar counter, toward a door in the back. Evan watched him but did nothing to stop him. When the man had left the room, Evan went in the door after him. He didn't want a room full of witnesses for what he was about to do.

The door the man left through led to a small corridor leading to what Evan assumed was a staff room or storage. The man was not too far ahead of him, his back turned to the door as he lit a cigarette. He had no time to turn around as Evan shoved him in the back. He smacked against the wall of the corridor, dropping his lighter, which sputtered out as it clattered to the ground. Evan pressed his elbow into the man's back.

"I don't recognize you, but you're a shifter. I can smell it. Who are you, and how do you know Al?"

The man wheezed and Evan smacked the wall a mere inch from his face.

"Go to hell," the man spat.

Evan wrenched the man's arm up behind his back. The man squealed in pain but the music in the other room drowned out his cries. "You're going to tell me what I want to know, or it's going to get a lot worse."

"Okay, okay," the man yielded but Evan did not loosen the pressure on his arm. The man replied through gritted teeth. "I'm a drifter, I'm not from here. Al was selling me a place in his pride if I did some stuff for him."

Evan raised the man's arm higher. His breaths came out ragged but he kept talking. "The girl, he wanted to use my apartment to keep her for a while. Said he needed a nice quiet place to do business. No one knows I work for him so it was the perfect hiding place."

"Where?" Evan growled.

"Atwater Village. If you let me go I can write it down for you."

Evan released the man. He took a small notepad and pen from his bartender's apron and scribbled down an address. "Here," he shoved the paper at Evan. "Can I go now?"

"Yeah, you can go. But if I see you in this city again you're dead," Evan warned. The man nodded jerkily and ran away down the hall. Evan went back into the club.

"So, you know where she is?" Tessa asked as soon as she saw Evan.

"Yeah," Evan replied. "I don't think we have much time. Let's go."

It was the dead of night when they got to the bartender's apartment. The street was as silent as the grave and there was no traffic on the streets. Evan knew the neighborhood to be heavy with gang activity, the perfect place for Al to bring a kidnapped woman without being noticed. The building that matched the address was four stories with no elevator.

He and Tessa had to walk up three flights of stairs to get to the apartment. The green paint on the door was cracked and the zero in the middle of the number nailed to the door was missing. A faint halo of faded paint marked where the number once was.

Evan had told Tess to wait in the car, but she insisted on coming with him. She kept her hand near the gun by her hip, which was mostly hidden by the hem of her leather jacket.

"You ready?" he said to her, not knowing what would meet them on the other side of the door.

She nodded. He knocked, ready to bust in as soon as someone opened the door.

It was Al who was the unlucky victim. As soon as Evan saw that head of greasy hair appear through the crack in the door, he shoved his full weight into the door sending it flying open. Al tumbled out of the way, and in an instant Evan could see that Lily was not in the apartment. He shouted her name but there was no answer. Evan felt disappointment which turned quickly into a burning rage.

Before Al could react, Evan swung at his jaw and felt a sickening crack on impact. Al toppled to the ground and Evan bore down on him, his fists pummeling the man's face relentlessly. All that was going through Evan's mind was the desire to hurt Al and the need for retribution in Lily's name.

"Evan!" Tessa screamed.

Evan turned to see her pointing her gun shakily at a man who had just come out of the bathroom.

"Whoa," the man said, holding his hands up in front of him. "Tell your girl to drop the gun."

Tessa looked ready to shoot, so Evan told the man, "Go back in the bathroom and lock the door. Stay in there until we're done. I can't be responsible for what happens if you don't."

The man retreated into the bathroom and Evan heard the lock click. He instructed Tessa, "Keep the gun pointed at the door. If he tries to come out, shoot him."

Tessa nodded, her eyes wide. She kept the gun trained on the door, just as Evan told her.

Al's head lolled from side to side as blood dribbled from his nose and mouth. Evan got off him and dragged him into a sitting position with his back against the wall.

"Where's Lily?"

Al closed his eyes. Evan slapped his cheek a few times. Al's eyes snapped open and he moaned in pain. Evan repeated the question.

"Desert," he mumbled through his split lip.

"Where in the desert?" Evan growled.

Al's eyes rolled back in his head. Evan only slightly regretted beating him as much as he had. Evan grabbed a glass of water from a nearby table and splashed him with it. Al sputtered and his eyes flew open. He sat straight up.

Evan told him, "Your friend in the bathroom's not the only one at risk of getting a bullet through him. Now tell me what I want to know."

Al spat a glob of blood from his mouth and answered. "East, out by Joshua Tree. There's that big empty patch off the side of the highway. She wouldn't do what we wanted so we left her there to die."

Evan swallowed back the bile in his throat. Al was truly disgusting. Evan stood and stepped away from Al. As he did so, his foot kicked something hard that rolled along the floor before coming to a stop by the table. He leaned down and picked it up. It was a syringe with a few drops of yellow still clinging to the needle.

"She didn't want to take her medicine," Al chuckled.

Evan looked at Al with murder in his eyes and was about to attack again, but Tessa stopped him. "Evan, we don't have time. We have to get to Lily."

"We're not done," Evan warned Al before following Tessa out the door.

THE FINAL CHAPTER

The fuel gauge had been hovering on empty for quite some time, but Evan tried to ignore it as if through sheer will alone he would be able to keep the car going all the way to Joshua Tree. Tessa had fallen silent. Dawn would be upon them soon enough, though the sky was still dark and foreboding as Evan drove east away from the city and farther into the desert.

"We'll find her, you know," Evan said, as much for his own sake as Tessa's.

"That's not what I'm worried about," Tessa replied. "It's what state we'll find her in when we do that's got me nervous."

Evan felt the same way, but he didn't want to put a voice to his concerns, as if saying them out loud would turn them to reality.

"The desert is really big," Tessa said. "You know, back when we still lived in Nevada Lily always used to say that she was meant for something bigger. I doubt this was what she meant." Tessa fell silent for a while, looking out the window. She sighed. "You know, you're like a dream come to life for her.

Moving to the big city and falling in love with a Hollywood star, one with a hidden power almost too insane to believe. And now here you come to save the day in her darkest hour. You'd better be ready to spend the rest of your life with her."

"Actually, that's exactly what I intend," Evan said, watching the road with a serious expression. "As long as she'll have me back."

Tessa humphed in satisfaction and settled back in her seat. She glanced over at Evan with a look of appraisal in her eyes. "I'll put in a good word for you," she said.

The car started to shake and sputter. Its last reserves of fuel had been used up and it was now running on fumes. Evan took his foot off the gas pedal and edged the car off the road, parking it on the dirt shoulder of the two-lane highway. They were still about forty minutes out from Joshua Tree, and maybe twenty from the place Al had said they had abandoned Lily.

Evan smacked the horn, the sharp sounds disturbing the otherwise quiet stretch of road. He hunched over the steering wheel, his arms crossed over it and his forehead resting on his arms in a gesture of failure.

"We're out of gas," he mumbled.

He heard the car door open and Tessa got out of the car. "Get your ass out here, prince charming," she snapped at him.

He reluctantly forced himself out of the car. He had failed Lily yet again, so close to saving her too. They would now have to wait until morning when they could call a tow truck, or find someone to give them a ride back into the city for gas. Twenty minutes in the car on the highway was an impossible distance on foot.

Tessa asked him, "How fast can lions run?"

Evan asked her to repeat the question, not sure what it had to do with their current situation.

"How fast can lions run?"

Evan shrugged.

"Lions chase down things like zebras and gazelles, right? You guys must be able to run fast, and pretty far too. I doubt not having a car's gonna stop you from getting to Lily."
Evan looked up at Tessa as the corners of his mouth curled into a smile. "You're right," he said.

Maybe as a man he was no match for the desert, but as a lion, he could cover a lot of ground in a short time. He wasted no time pulling off his shirt, and was about to do the same with his pants when Tessa stopped him.

"Whoa, hold on there," she said. "Let me at least turn around first. I'm sure you look great naked and all, but I'm gonna let Lily keep the privilege of seeing you like that to herself."

Evan couldn't help but laugh despite his anxiety to find Lily. He discarded his clothes and transformed into his lion form in privacy.

Tessa turned around again only when she heard him growl. She gasped, the easy confidence of her usual demeanor gone in a flash as she stood face to face with a lion for the first time. He tried to look less ferocious, but was not sure how to manage that. On all four paws he was only as high as her chest, but he knew the combination of his long mane and large canine teeth made quite the impression.

But Evan had no time to waste letting Tessa adjust to his new appearance. He turned and ran off into the desert, using his animal instincts to guide him and leaving Tessa stuttering after him.

"Yeah, you go find Lily and I'll—I'll just wait here in the car."

Her voice was soon lost to the silence of the night and the soft crunch of desert sand under his paws. He tried to pick up Lily's scent on the breeze, moving his head from side to side and adjusting his run towards where he sensed it was the strongest. The scent was so faint that he might have been imagining it, but he stayed on course trusting his instincts to find her.

The stars started to dim and the moon became a ghost of itself as the sun began its slow climb over the horizon. Back in the city the lights were blinking out, their nighttime brilliance overshadowed by the breaking dawn.

Crawling insects retreated back under their rocks to escape the coming sun and its scorching heat.

Lily sat where she had for most of the night, her lips dry and cracking though her skin was clammy with sweat.

She whispered to herself over and over that when the sun came up, she would be saved. Anything to battle the storm clouds that the drugs were leaving in their wake. The sky turned from pitch black to a deep blue and in the distance, a shadow took shape against the desert landscape.

Lily looked up, sensing something else out there in the desert with her. At first she thought she was hallucinating the beast coming towards her. It was a lion running at her in the California desert, the only thing moving for miles in the barren wasteland of sand and dry brush. It made easy progress over the uneven ground, its gait never wavering as it approached.

Lily hugged her knees and buried her head in her lap. She scrunched her eyes together and told the vision to go away. But when she looked up again it was still there, like the shadow of death on the red-tinged horizon.

Lily stood, but her legs were too weak and she stumbled and fell. In frustration, she pounded the dirt around her, her fists raising up little clouds of dust. In the growing light, she could see the streaks of dirt across her skin and the yellowing bruise on the inside of her elbow from where the needle had done its work. As she sat in the dirt marveling over the sickly tone bubbling out against her tan skin, the lion came to a stop in front of her.

She was afraid to touch it, as if doing so would make the mirage disappear in a shimmer of air. It was hard to tell what was real. Had she really been kidnapped, or was that a dream, too?

Tentatively, she held out her hand and the lion came forward to meet it. She stroked its snout, feeling the short, bristly fur between her fingers. She then moved her hand up between its ears and into its mane, growing more sure of her senses with every touch.

Twining her fingers in the luxurious crown of fur, she told herself this was real. She may not have been able to trust her eyes, but she knew she could trust her sense of touch. The lion licked at the side of her face, its tongue rough like a cat's but warm and comforting against Lily's tear-streaked cheek. She started to cry.

"I'm sorry," she sobbed, recognizing Evan through the mask of his animal form. She wrapped her arms around the beast's neck, burying her face in the soft fur of its mane. "I shouldn't have doubted you. You were tricked and so was I. I wish I could have told you I loved you before—"

The lion in her arms dissolved away, leaving only the man she loved. Lily faded in and out of consciousness, barely aware of the voice telling her everything would be okay. She wanted to believe it, she really did. But everything seemed so irrevocably damaged. She had seen a side of the city she had never wanted to, and it would never be the same for her again.

"Lily, are you okay? Are you hurt?" Evan tried to get a good look at her face, but she writhed away suddenly feeling like his eyes were burning her.

"Lily, can you understand me?"

Her grasp on reality was trying to get away from her and she was struggling to keep hold of it. Was the man who held her in his arms a friend or was he trying to hurt her again? Lily twisted away and fell in the dirt.

"It's okay. I'm here." His arms wrapped around her again. Evan hugged her protectively, letting her fall against him as the last of her strength gave out.

"Please," she whimpered as Evan held her close. "Please take me away from here."

"I will," Evan reassured in a soothing tone. "I will."

He held her close as the sun climbed up over the horizon, its orange rays piercing through the last bits of darkness and bathing everything in a warm glow. Evan looked down to Lily whose eyes were closed. She looked peaceful. *She had missed the sunrise again*, Evan thought.

He lifted her limp body off the ground and carried her back towards the road. When he was in sight of the long ribbon of blacktop he stopped and called Tessa to tell her he had Lily, and that she was safe. Tessa told him she had found gas and would come and pick him up. He lifted Lily back up in his arms and carried her to the edge of the road where they waited for Tessa to come.

The sun was starting to warm Lily's clammy skin, and her eyes fluttered open. She looked afraid and Evan soothed her, whispering to her that she was safe and that he would protect her.

Tessa pulled up just as Lily slipped out of consciousness again. She got out of the car and helped Evan get Lily into the back.

"Will she be okay?" Tessa asked, looking at her shivering friend with concern.

"She'll be fine once we get her home," Evan replied taking the keys from Tessa and sliding into the driver's seat.

"Shouldn't we take her to the hospital?"

"She's been drugged. They'll ask questions, ones which we don't have easy answers for. She just needs to sleep it off. I promise I'll take good care of her. My brother had a nasty drug habit, and I know how to take care of someone who's crashing. By the way," Evan said as he started the long drive back to the city. "How'd you get the gas?"

"I flagged down a passing big rig and the driver let me siphon enough gas to get us home. He said he liked your car, and it was a pity to see it stuck on the side of the road like that. I guess it's a good thing you drive an antique."

Were he any less exhausted, Evan would have had a comeback for Tessa's jab at his car, but the long night and relief at having found Lily was finally catching up to him. He glanced in the rearview mirror at Lily asleep in the back seat.

She looked peaceful for now, but Evan knew what hell was still in store for her. There was no doubt Al had used a nasty mix of drugs on her. Evan would deal with Al later, and Darien, too.

When they got back to Lily and Tessa's apartment, Evan helped Lily stagger to the bed. She was conscious, but only barely. She did not seem to know where she was, and her body was shaking violently with chills. Evan peeled the dirty clothes from her body, the fabric cold and damp from her sweat, and wiped her down with a wet towel to both soothe her discomfort and wash away the desert sand.

When she was clean he pulled the covers up over her and let her sleep, though Evan himself stayed awake at her bedside. Exhausted as he was, he needed to take care of Lily. Tessa had offered to help, but Evan knew he had to make up for what he had dragged her into. It was his duty.

Sometimes she clutched his hand almost painfully and other times she cried out in her sleep. Every time Lily awoke, however briefly, Evan patiently got her to drink a few sips of water to battle the dehydration she was no doubt suffering. Tessa came in a couple of times, but mostly left Evan to it. She understood his need to prove his devotion to Lily, to be the one at her bedside when she finally woke up.

Late into the day, Evan found himself dozing. He sat up straight and looked towards Lily. Lily shifted in her sleep and muttered something incoherent. Her eyebrows furrowed and she started to whimper. Evan wiped the cold sweat from her forehead with a wet towel and smoothed back her hair. She opened her eyes.

"Are you awake?" he asked.

"Mhmm," Lily replied. Her voice was no more than a weak whisper in her throat. Evan helped her drink some water.

"Nightmares, can't sleep," she mumbled. There were black circles under her eyes and the whites of her eyes were bloodshot.

Evan pulled off his dirt-stained jeans and crawled into bed next to her. Lily curled up against him, her naked body feeling much more frail than he remembered. He put his arm around her and kissed the top of her head.

"I'm here," he said.

"I know," Lily replied.

They lay for a while in each other's arms, Evan listening to the soft sigh of Lily's breath as her chest rose and fell under the covers.

"They gave me a choice," Lily said suddenly. "First it was Al, then Darien, but they told me what they would do to me if I didn't give in to what they wanted. And I still said no. I would have rather died than be forced to be with a man I didn't love."

Evan struggled to find the right words for what he needed to say. "I'm sorry I couldn't protect you," he said. "I'm sorry I didn't fight harder for you, and tell you how much you meant to me before all of this happened. You were strong for standing up to those men. Not many could have made the choice you did."

Lily shifted in bed, turning away from Evan. In a quiet voice, she said, "They told me why they were after me. And why you were, too. I was your prize to fight over. I couldn't let them take me like that."

Evan could only imagine what Lily thought of him. That she was even allowing him to touch her right now was a miracle. He was an animal, when it came down to it, ruled by instinct and the baser needs of survival. And what kind of woman would be able to love such a beast?

"But it's okay," Lily continued. "I know that Jade was a trick, and I want to believe you meant it when you said you loved me."

"I did, and I still do," Evan replied. "But you know what it means to be with me. You would have to become my mate. It's a big commitment, and one I'm willing to make with you. Of course, if that's something you want."

Evan felt Lily's hand find his under the covers. She guided it up over her breast and held it there. "I want to."

Understanding the full meaning of her words, Evan said. "But not now. You need rest."

Lily kept his hand where it was. "No, I only need you."

"Are you sure?"

"It will help me feel what's real again," she said as she turned to kiss him.

Her kiss was as exhilarating as their first, her tongue seeking out his as she pressed her body against him. Evan gently lowered her down onto her back as his mouth kept contact with hers.

"Let me take care of you," he said, his hand trailing softly down the line of her breasts to her stomach. As delicate as she was, he didn't want to hurt her. He would have to restrain that dominant, predatory part of himself and let Lily's body guide him instead.

He carefully parted her legs with his hand. She moaned in pleasure and closed her eyes. Kissing his way down, Evan peeled off his shirt before his head disappeared under the covers. His lips nibbled at her skin as his tongue tasted the sweetness of her sex. Even without being rough, he could still take command of her body, the pleasure alone driving Lily crazy and making her yearn for more of his touch.

"Please," Lily moaned as she pulled him up towards her. Her blue eyes met his amber ones and held them in her gaze. "I need you."

Evan reached down and guided himself between her legs. He could feel the heat of her against him even before he was inside. It was like a dream; after all this time she was accepting him as her mate. She was to be his lioness, the father of his children and the woman who would be by his side until he was old and grizzled.

She whimpered as he entered her and dug her fingers into his back. He went slowly, savoring the feeling of his skin against hers for the first time without a thin layer of latex keeping them apart. They were truly bonded now, in mind and body, and no one could take her away from him.

She held on to him tightly the whole time, as if scared he would leave her if she didn't. But he had no intention of ever leaving her again. The rhythm of his breaths matched hers in their quickening pace and he could feel her body tense. As she cried out his name, Evan looked into her eyes. He could see the future of his pride reflected back in them, a strong future for himself and Lily and the cubs she was soon to find herself pregnant with.

*

Lily was immensely nervous, though she had no reason at all to be so. She smoothed the waist of her sun dress and patted down her braided bun to make sure all the loose curls were accounted for. Evan stood next to her in a tuxedo, his arm around her waist as he smiled at the people taking pictures of the two of them.

"Are you okay?" Evan asked. "I know it's your first premier, but you don't have to be worried. The audience will love you, and even if they don't, I do. And that's the only thing that really matters."

"Your love won't help me pay for a new apartment," Lily said with a wry smile.

"You don't need a new apartment. You can live with me."

Since the night Evan had found her in the desert, Lily had not returned to her apartment. She was still helping Tessa pay the rent but she went home to Evan's place in Beverly Grove every night. Returning to her old neighborhood was too traumatic for her, and Evan worried that it was not safe either. Tessa was looking for a new place, too, and new roommates, knowing that Lily would not be coming back. It was looking like the end of their run together, best friends since childhood finally having grown old enough to say goodbye, at least for a little while.

Al and Darien had been laying low since the incident, but there was no telling when they would show their faces again. Evan said he had heard a rumor that the men had been cast from their pride by their true alpha. Lily wanted to believe the rumor more than anything, though it still wasn't enough. She loved LA, but she had seen its dark side. No amount of retribution would erase the bad memories that the city held for her.

But at least the movie was over, and after that she could close the book on this short, but turbulent time in her life. She had taken some time off to recover after her kidnapping, but by then principal photography had finished and she only needed to be available for pick-ups as needed.

While the film footage was busy being edited and polished for the movie screens, Lily had enjoyed some of the little things she and Evan had missed in their mess of a romance. He had taken her out to dinner, movies, and they had enjoyed together some of those comfortable silences that often settle over a happy couple. In short, she had been completely and utterly in love for perhaps the first time in her life.

And as her emotional wounds healed, so did Evan's physical ones. The scars he had sustained from his fights with Darien were ghosts of what they once were, only a slight sheen of taut white skin across his brow and in rows along his forearm where Darien's jaw had sunk in.Lily doubted that they would ever fully heal, but she saw them as a reminder of Evan's devotion to her and his willingness to protect her no matter what. Every time she noticed them again, it brought a small, knowing smile to her lips.

The director came walking up, looking a bit like a penguin in his tailored black suit. He looked around with bewilderment. "Evan, who are all these people?"

Evan gave him an innocent smile. "You said I could invite people."

"Yes, but I meant your parents or maybe a girlfriend. I didn't mean you could invite every person you know. The theater's not going to hold all of them."

Evan shrugged. "You'll find a way. I have faith in you."

The director gave Evan a searing look and stomped away in a huff, the sheen of sweat on the top of his balding head reflecting the lights of the marquis like a mirror.

"You should go easy on him," Lily said.

"I am," Evan replied. "You should have seen how I treated him on our first movie together. I was horrible, though to be fair I was a young kid who thought he ruled the world. But he said he liked my fighting spirit, so I can't really disappoint him now, can I?"

Evan gave a bashful smile, at least as bashful as a man like him could manage, and Lily smiled back. She knew the director was almost single-handedly responsible for making Evan's career, and that the two were quite close, despite appearances. The mutual antagonism was just each man's way of showing he cared for the other. Lily, as a woman, could not quite understand it but she appreciated it nonetheless.

Luckily for Lily, the director was nothing but sweet to her and he was already thinking of a place for her in his next film. There was no doubt she would be starring alongside Evan again, which she didn't mind one bit.

"By the way," Lily said, looking around at the people milling about on the red carpet outside the theater, "I don't recognize any of these people. Are they show business friends of yours? They sure don't look like actors and actresses."

Though well-dressed, much of the crowd looked like they had never been to an event like this one. Some kept to themselves, looking like a deer in the headlights whenever a camera flashed near them, and others chatted away loudly in a manner better fitting a baseball stadium than a movie premier's red carpet.

Lily caught sight of one man she recognized. He was older, perhaps in his sixties, and despite his beer belly, Lily could see that he had once been quite handsome in his youth. She couldn't figure out why she recognized him, though, and the thought nagged her. If he was someone important in Hollywood it would be rude of her not to at least say hello.

She asked Evan, "Who's that man standing over there?"

Evan looked to where Lily was indicating.

The man noticed them looking at him and put a hand up to shield his eyes from the low evening sun at their backs. It was then Lily's memory came back to her. He was the man from the café by her apartment on the day she had been stalked by Darien.

He had been wearing a Dodgers cap that day, and that was why Lily couldn't quite place him. But seeing him with his hand over his brow casting a shadow like the bill of a baseball cap brought Lily's recollections flooding back.

Whoever he was, he must have meant trouble. It was no coincidence that she would see him here after all that had happened.

He started walking over and Evan waved in encouragement.

"What are you doing?" Lily hissed in a panicked voice.

"Don't worry, it's only my dad."

"Your dad? He was following me in my neighborhood. Tessa kept saying she'd seen him around and I saw him watching us in a café one time. I thought he had something to do with Darien."

Evan laughed. "He was only making sure you were good enough for his son. I'm sure he's sorry if he made you uneasy."

Lily felt only momentary relief before her nerves came back for an entirely different reason. She was about to meet Evan's dad, the man who was set to become her father-in-law once the promotional tour for their movie was over and they had enough time for themselves to get a wedding planned.

Lily wondered if the man even knew they were engaged. Lily felt like she should have prepared more for this moment, all her words flying out of her head in a panic. She feared she would make a terrible first impression.

The man walked up to them before Lily could regain composure.

"Dad, meet Lily. And Lily, meet my dad," Evan introduced the two.

Evan's dad put his hand out to shake and Lily gave a second of pause before accepting it. His shake was firm but not unkind. He smiled at her.

"It's nice to finally see this woman my son's so crazy about."

Evan coughed. "Dad, she knows about the, um, she saw you following her."

Lily tried to protest, but Evan's words were already out in the air. He had seen the elephant in the room and shot it dead in one sentence. Lily felt like she could die of embarrassment.

The man scratched the back of his head in a very Evan-like gesture. "Oh hell, I'm so sorry. I'm sure with everything that was going on at the time, you were scared out of your wits when you saw me just now. If there's anything I can do to make it up to you," he said, thrusting his hands nervously into his pockets.

"It's okay," Lily said, her voice only slightly wavering. "Really. I'm just glad I can finally meet you." Relief washed over her as she managed to get the words out.

"I can see why you like her," he said to Evan.

Evan put his arm around Lily's waist. "I'm a very lucky man," he replied.

Evan's dad turned to Lily, "So what's this Evan's been telling me about an engagement ring?"

Lily blushed and Evan put a finger to his lips. He said, "We haven't told anyone yet. We don't want the movie's opening to be overshadowed by talk of our wedding. I'm pretty sure the director would kill me if I took the spotlight from him. He may not look it, but he's quite the diva."

Lily laughed, knowing that Evan was making a joke. The real reason they were keeping it a secret was that they wanted some time to themselves without the cameras all over them. Even Evan was nowhere near the level of celebrity that had paparazzi hounding him at every turn, but she knew that one rumor of onscreen romance turned real would have the reporters at their door in an instant.

Everyone liked Hollywood romance, though most were just waiting to see it fail. She didn't want their love to become a spectacle to be sold on the covers of magazines. That was not the kind of fame she was after.

"Well, don't take too long," Evan's dad said. "Because Lily's going to have a hard time walking down the aisle with a baby in her arms."

"You told him I'm pregnant?" Lily asked Evan in shock. She had been hoping to make the announcement together, sometime after she had had a chance to meet the members of his pride and introduce herself as his fiancée.

Evan winced from her tone and scratched the back of his head just as his father had done moments earlier. "Sorry, I was too excited. I couldn't help it. I called him as soon as you told me, and I might

232

have told my brother and a few other members of the pride as well. It's just been a while since we've had new cubs in the family and my brother has the only one. Family's important to the pride."

Lily begrudgingly forgave him. She was looking forward to becoming a part of his pride and his family. There was a whole world of shifters that she had only scratched the surface of. She couldn't wait to learn all she could about him and his pride, and she had her whole life ahead of her to do so.

There was one loose end Evan still had to clear up. He went to see Youssef at his office as soon as he heard the man had been released from the hospital. Youssef's office was on the top floor of a small strip club he owned in downtown LA, a place where the dancing women and smoky bar were mostly a front for more illicit activities happening in the back rooms.

The building itself was painted black on the outside, with silver silhouettes of women painted in sexy poses. Even from afar, it was easy to see what kind of business it was. When Evan went inside, his eyes had trouble adjusting to the dark after the bright August sunshine outside and for a moment, everything was black.

Little by little he could start to make out the shapes of waitresses passing by with trays of drinks and the few lonely men sitting in front of the stage, where women lazily moved their half-naked bodies for tips that would barely pay the bills. But Evan had absolutely no interest in the women, or the money they weren't earning.

There was one thing on his mind, Lily, and more specifically her safety. He could not rest until he knew what really happened to the two men who had hurt her so much. He needed to know they were getting what they deserved.

Youssef's office on the top floor could be accessed from a staircase carpeted in pink shag whose walls were lined with pinup posters from what looked like the fifties. On the door to the office at the top was a framed picture of Youssef from days long past, his full head of hair and winning smile giving a very different impression from what one expected to find within.

The office contained more of the awful pink carpeting, plus an expensive-looking wooden desk and matching leather chair in which the man himself sat. Evan found the whole place both gaudy and cliché, but the pride raked in a good amount of money from their backroom deals and under-the-table sales. But Evan was not concerned with Youssef's place of business. He was here to talk about Darien, and his would-be usurper Al.

Youssef sat at his desk, his suit looking two sizes too big for his frail frame. He gestured for Evan to sit at a chair facing his desk, looking Evan over as if he had been expecting him for quite some time.

"I'm glad to see you're feeling better," Evan said, feeling pleasantries were in order after the debt he owed the old man for having been the voice of reason in all the chaos. It was good to know there was at least one member of the rival pride who had Lily's best interests at heart.

"You're here to talk about what happened, aren't you?" Youssef asked.

Evan replied, "I need to know what happened to Darien, and Al. I need to know that Lily's safe."

The old man nodded. "You tell me what happened that night, and then we'll talk. I've only gotten the story from the mouths of the guilty. I need confirmation that my judgment is sound."

Youssef kept his hands clasped under his chin as if in prayer as he listened to Evan explain everything that had happened. The man's shoulders were slumped and his cheeks were more hollow than they had been before his heart attack. He looked small in the big leather chair he sat in, almost like a child playing at being a businessman.

But Evan knew that inside he was the same old cutthroat he used to be. Years had only softened the edges.

"I'm sure you already know Al's been forced to leave the pride," Youssef said when Evan had finished talking. "I'm sorry I wasn't able to deal with him more harshly, but his mother begged me to spare him. She's old and he's her only son. Al took the news hard, and tore up the bar where he used to do most of his bookkeeping. He burned all the records and took the money with him.

"Then he went south of the border where I've heard he has friends in the cartels down there. There's no chance he's coming back, and if he does, we'll deal with him ourselves. After all, he's our responsibility. I should have kept a closer eye on him from the start."

"And your son?" Evan asked, not failing to catch Youssef's omission. "I've heard he's been kicked out along with Al, but somehow I don't believe it."

Youssef closed his eyes with a look of regret. When he opened them again it appeared as if there were tears in them. Evan had underestimated how much the years had really softened the old man.

"He's my son. I know what I told you in the hospital, but it's not so easy to turn your back on family as I thought.

I'm not going to be around much longer, according to the doctors, and I don't want to squander what little time I have left. I already have my successor in place, a young man who's already got a mate of his own. The rest of the pride have assured me they won't let my son challenge the boy for dominance after I'm gone. As for Darien himself, I'm keeping him on a short leash. He won't go near your girl again. You have my word."

"You know we can't forgive him for what he did," Evan said, thinking mostly of Lily and the trauma she suffered at Darien, and Al's, hands.

The old man let his hands fall into his lap. "And I'm not asking you to. I'm only telling you what I've done to try to make up for my pride's mistakes. All I ask is that you don't try to take matters into your own hands. We've all suffered enough."

"But what about Lily?" Evan asked, anger rising in his voice though he tried to control it. "She can't move on knowing he's still out there. Even if you tell us she's safe, there's no way she'll believe it unless Darien is off the streets of LA."

Youssef replied with calm in the face of Evan's anger. "Then it might be better if you leave LA, just for a while," he said. "You know my pride has nothing without this city, otherwise we would leave it to you instead."

237

Evan thought about leaving Los Angeles, the only city he had ever known and the place he loved despite all its flaws. Youssef said his pride had nothing without the city, but Evan felt the same way. The city was a part of him, and he wasn't sure who he was without it. But if it was better for Lily, he would make the sacrifice.

"There's plenty of space to roam north of here," Youssef said. "And there aren't any other prides that way. You won't have problems like you did here. No one will be after Lily. You'll be able to live your lives in peace."

That wasn't what Evan was worried about. He was worried about leaving his home, and the backlash he would receive from the rest of the pride for even trying to suggest such a thing. He knew his father would be the worst of them, and most of the older generation would side with him, too.

Evan wasn't sure he even wanted to convince them, but he had to think of Lily and of the cubs she was carrying. No matter what, Evan didn't want them to have to experience the same kind of childhood he had. He wanted them safe from the influences of gangs, drugs, and the other kinds of trouble a young lion could get into on the streets of LA.

Evan thanked the man for his time and excused himself from the office. Though it was still only mid-afternoon, the place was already starting to get busy. For every man that plunked himself down by the stage, another two or three entered an unmarked door leading to the back.

Their dark shades and low caps told Evan they were not here for the girls. It was likely the briefcases they carried held large sums of money. Evan had to remind himself that no matter how much Youssef's word meant, or how much he helped Evan, he was still a common criminal at the end of the day. Did Evan really want to keep living in a place where his and Lily's safety was dependent on such a man's promises? He told himself he would start looking at properties outside the city tomorrow. If he kept things modest, he might just have enough money to help his entire pride relocate to the suburbs. The hardest part would be convincing them.

****

It had been almost a year since they had moved out of Los Angeles. The green vistas of northern California were suiting them a lot better than the sprawling concrete jungle they had come from. There was more room out here for the cubs, and the pride didn't have to worry about trouble from other shifters. Few drifters passed their way through here, and when they did, they were usually on their way to somewhere else.

For the most part, Lily and Evan had given up their lives in Hollywood, but they didn't need the fame to keep themselves happy. Every day surrounded by their family and friends was more than enough for the two of them. That and the knowledge that their sons would grow up far from the dangerous streets of downtown Los Angeles where their father and mother had nearly lost each other all those years ago.

Now, Evan and Lily's pride was able to thrive in their own wide territory with little to worry about, besides, of course, the cubs getting out and startling the neighbors. Which had happened on a couple of occasions already. Though only three years old, the pair was already a handful.

Lily watched the twins tussle on the grass together, their tiny tufted tails whipping wildly as they pounced on each other and yelped in glee. The high hedge surrounding their property kept them from prying eyes, though most of the neighbors were members of Evan's own pride so the risk was very low. Evan's dad sat on the porch steps with a beer in his hand, egging on the little ones as if he were at a boxing match.

Already, Lily could see that they would be as tough as their father when they grew up. She was not looking forward to the day when the twins would have to decide which one of them would take over for their father and become alpha.

Evan's dad put down his beer can and jumped in to join the boys' fight. They immediately let go of each other and started attacking their grandfather with ferocity. His booming laugh echoed across the lawn.

Evan's dad had been the most reluctant to relocate, though he was taking well to his new surroundings. The old man was set in his ways and had at first despised the idea of living anywhere besides the home of the Dodgers, his favorite baseball team. But like it or not, Evan was the alpha, and he had made the final decision to move the pride out to a different part of the state.

The old man had had no choice but to pack up his things and move out with the rest of them. But after seeing what life was like without all the violence and corruption around them, Evan's dad was now glad they had made the move. His grandchildren would have a chance to grow up without many of the struggles his own children faced. And in that, he was a happy grandfather.

"Okay, grandpa, time to go inside," Lily called. "We need to get the cubs washed up before dinner."

The old man reluctantly stood, grabbing a wriggling cub under each arm and walking them towards the house.

Lily stopped them at the door. "And what's the policy about lions inside the house?" she asked with a stern look.

The boys transformed back, allowing Lily to see the full extent of their filth. Dirt smeared their rosy cheeks, and their elbows and knees were green with grass stains. The wavy brown hair they had inherited from their father was hopelessly tangled. She would have to scrub them in the bath before letting them sit at the dinner table with the rest of the family. She told them to go wait for her in the bathroom.

Inside, the rich smell of spaghetti sauce and garlic bread filled the house. Matt's wife, Kat, came in with a stack of plates as Lily entered the dining room. Matt sat at the large table next to his six-year-old son, who was only now getting the hang of being able to sit through dinner with the grownups.

The boy looked like a miniature of his father and was much more quiet than her own sons. He may not ever become alpha, but he would become a strong member of the pride, nonetheless.

Evan came up from behind Lily and wrapped his arms around her.

"I need to give the cubs a bath," she said. "Granddad was teaching them how to wrestle outside and they're covered in dirt."

"Do you think they'll be able to beat me some day?" Evan asked.

"Not for a long while," Lily replied. "Whether you like it or not, you're stuck leading this pride until you're old and grey."

Evan smiled. "It's not so bad as long as I've got you by my side."

Lily disentangled herself from her husband's embrace and went to deal with the cubs. One of them had turned on the bathtub tap by himself and was splashing the walls with muddy water. The other had apparently forgotten his mother's strict rule about shifting inside the house and was busy tearing apart the toilet paper roll with his tiny claws.

"Okay you two, it's bath time."

At seeing his angry mother in the doorway, the cub promptly turned back into a human boy with a look of guilt in his blue eyes. Lily scooped him up and put him in the bath with his brother.

By the time the cubs were clean, Lily was drenched with bath water and exhausted. Kat came in from the hallway. "I'll take the little ones. You can come to the table when you're ready. No rush."

Lily was glad to have someone around who understood the unique struggle of raising shifter cubs. Like Lily, Matt's wife was also a non-shifter. They had met when Kat was a waitress at a café Matt liked to go to. She had been as surprised as Lily at finding out her husband's secret, but her love for him was stronger than her reservations about marrying such a man.

Kat lent a helping hand whenever Lily needed it, which was quite often, as her twins were little furry balls of pure energy. They would have destroyed the house by now had Lily not set down the rule about no lions allowed inside. Even so, they slipped up occasionally.

After Kat left with the boys, Evan came in closing the door behind him. He smoothed back Lily's hair and helped her out of her soaking wet shirt.

"Thank you for taking care of the boys," he said.

Lily sighed and leaned into Evan's chest. His arms went around her.

"I'm doing okay, right?"

He lifted her chin and gave her a long, drawn-out kiss. Lily's eyes fluttered closed as she lost herself in his embrace. He kissed her again, more deeply, his tongue seeking out hers as his hands moved to her waist.

"They're waiting for us," Lily breathed. "We should go."

Evan only kissed her harder, his mouth finding the sensitive spot behind her ear and moving downwards to her neck. There was nothing Lily could do but give in to his touch, her own body powerless to the desire she felt for him.

"Okay, but you have to be quick," she whispered as she wriggled up onto the bathroom counter.

"Whatever you want, I'm yours," Evan replied as he ran his hand through her hair.
He gave Lily a kiss and she felt that shiver of excitement that never left her no matter how much time they were together.

Each day she fell in love with him again, and each day their bond grew stronger. It may have been instinct that had brought them together, but it was mutual love and understanding that kept them there. And Lily planned to be there for a long while yet.

THE END

Message To YOU From Lilly Pink:

*Thanks so much for reading all the way to the end, I really hope you enjoyed it. If you want you can check out all my other **LION** shifter books by going to my __Amazon page here.__*

By the way, if you really did love it then I hope you can please give me a rating as it is a big help to independent authors like myself. :)

Get Yourself a FREE Bestselling Paranormal Romance Book!

Join the "**Simply Shifters**" Mailing list today and gain access to an exclusive **FREE** classic Paranormal Shifter Romance book by one of our bestselling authors along with many others more to come. You will also be kept up to date on the best book deals in the future on the hottest new Paranormal Romances. We are the HOME of Paranormal Romance after all!

* Get FREE Shifter Romance Books For Your Kindle & Other Cool giveaways

* Discover Exclusive Deals & Discounts Before Anyone Else!

* Be The FIRST To Know about Hot New Releases From Your Favorite Authors

Click The Link Below To Access Get All This Now!

SimplyShifters.com

Already subscribed?
OK, *Turn The Page!*

ALSO BY SIMPLY SHIFTERS....

SIMPLY WERELIONS
A TEN BOOK WERELION ROMANCE COLLECTION

50% DISCOUNT!!

Love Hunky WereLions? This is an excellent opportunity to own 10 Best Selling Lion Shifter Romance Books In One Limited Edition Digital Boxed Set.

1 Bonnie Burrows – The Lion's Shared Bride
2 Jade White – The Lion's Love Child
3 Jasmine White – The Roar Of The Lioness
4 Lilly Pink – The Lion's Heir
5 Angela Foxxe – Lions Surrogate
6 Maria Amor – The PlayLion
7 JJ Jones – Chained To The Lion
8 Ellie Valentina – Shared By The Lions (unreleased)
9 Lilly Pink – A Wild Time
10 Amira Rain – Melted By The Lion

START READING NOW AT THE BELOW LINK!

Amazon.com > http://www.amazon.com/Simply-Lions-Paranormal-WereLion-Collection-ebook/dp/B01BC47KBE/

Amazon UK > http://www.amazon.co.uk/Simply-Lions-Paranormal-WereLion-Collection-ebook/dp/B01BC47KBE/

Amazon Australia > http://www.amazon.com.au/Simply-Lions-Paranormal-WereLion-Collection-ebook/dp/B01BC47KBE/

Amazon Canada > http://www.amazon.ca/Simply-Lions-Paranormal-WereLion-Collection-ebook/dp/B01BC47KBE/